THE FINAL HARVEST

To: Peder

Alyre Caissie

ALYRE CAISSIE

ILLUSTRATIONS BY RACHELLE DESMEULES

THE FINAL HARVEST

Copyright © 2010 Alyre Caissie

All rights reserved. No part of this publication may be reproduced, stored in a retrieval system, or transmitted in any form or by any means—electronic, mechanical, photocopying, recording, or any other—except for brief quotations in printed reviews, without the prior written consent of the copyright owner or publisher. Any unauthorized publication is an infringement of the copyright law.

This book is a work of fiction. Names, characters, places, and incidents are the product of the author's imagination or are used fictitiously.

ISBN-13: 978-1-77069-106-3

Printed in Canada.

Word Alive Press
131 Cordite Road, Winnipeg, Manitoba, R3W 1S1
www.wordalivepress.ca

WORD ALIVE PRESS
Just Write!

Mixed Sources
Cert no. SW-COC-001271
© 1996 FSC
FSC

Library and Archives Canada Cataloguing in Publication

Caissie, Alyre, 1964-
   The final harvest / written by Alyre Caissie ; illustrated by Rachelle Desmeules.

ISBN 978-1-77069-106-3

   1. Christian fiction, Canadian (English). I. Desmeules, Rachelle II. Title.

PS8605.A42F56 2010   C813'.6   C2010-906170-5

Acknowledgments

I wish to thank Jacqui Hopper for not giving up on me throughout this project. Without her ghost writing, as she calls it, writing this project would have taken a lot longer. I would also like to thank Word Alive Press for believing in the book.

Preface

In Revelation 12:11, God reveals to us that there is a time coming on the earth when we as believers will overcome the enemy by the Blood of the Lamb and by the word of our testimony. In Matthew 9:35–37, Jesus talks of a sheep without a shepherd and how they were harassed by the enemy and helpless without Him. We understand the parallel that God made between sheep and people and Christ as the Good Shepherd.

In Matthew 9:37, Jesus referred to this parallel as the harvest fields. The fictional stories found in The Final Harvest, as in the parable of the lost sheep, are stories of people who took God at His Word and overcame the enemy of their soul.

We at Building The House Productions are working on converting the first two stories of this novel into a motion picture, with the intention of turning the remaining five stories into a mini-series.

We would like to hear from you in response to *The Final Harvest*, and hope that you would keep us in prayer as we follow the leading of God. If *The Final Harvest* has blessed you and you would like to share your testimony, please feel free to contact us. It may even be possible for a story to be written based on your experience

Please write to:
BUILDING THE HOUSE PRODUCTION
PO Box 40
Moncton NB E1C 8R9

Contents

The Harvest of Souls

by Dale Shannon

Hearing the voice of the Master
Telling the twelve on that day
That he would have to leave them
That he was going away

Through tears and hearts that were broken
Watching there lord disappear
Came a promise of one who would comfort
And make his purpose so clear

To the fields that are white onto harvest
Lost souls must be our goal
We must never be silent
Together for the harvest of souls

Day after day we're rejoicing
In all of God's riches we dwell
While people who live all around us
Without him are going to hell

Our comfort in Jesus is awesome
Our knowledge of God's word is the same
So why do we choose to be silent
And never speak in his name

Broken…. Bleeding and dying
Breathing his last on the cross
Jesus thought not of his own life
But wanted to harvest the lost

As sheep who know the master
We know those not in the fold
We must have the heart of the shepherd
And not rest until they are told

Introduction

A New Start

Cold, soaked through to the marrow of her bones, Jane Dorey dashed with almost practiced precision through the door of the first restaurant en route to her destination. Shivering and dripping large drops of rain water on the freshly scrubbed tile floor around her feet, she glanced around the nearly empty dining area and smiled with reminiscent familiarity.

Had it only been two days ago she'd indulged herself with chocolate cheesecake and equally delicious eavesdropping? And what a conversation it'd been!

The slap of April showers against the picture window pushed her towards the same corner table she'd occupied forty eight hours earlier. Before sitting down, she shook off the yellow rain slicker and draped it across the back of the padded wooden chair.

"Hi. Nice day, huh?" The blonde waitress, in her trim white uniform, handed Jane a worn brown vinyl menu. Her greeting dripped with both sarcasm and friendliness. Just like that other time.

"Keep this up, and I'll need a boat," Jane quipped, matching the younger woman's light hearted banter.

"You're not kidding." The waitress shook out her short straight hair. "Can I get you anything to drink before you order?"

"Tea. Thanks." As the waitress walked away, Jane was again struck by the sameness between this day and the other. Only Jane knew she wasn't the same woman who'd sat down at this table that other time.

That other Jane had been overwhelmed with overdue bills, running the kids to various sports events, and trying to keep her marriage from unraveling. That other Jane had sat like a wilted promise of what could have been; ready to walk away from everything that once upon a time she'd held close to her heart; family, friends, home...

Over time, she'd given away every piece of herself to others, and now she had nothing. Was nothing. Hopelessness pressed down on her shoulders, crushing her face down into the rubble of what had become her life.

While she'd wallowed in her silent sorrow, one of the two women at the next table had discussed a topic that had brought Jane's head up slowly, the words inflating her soul with something she hadn't felt in years; hope.

"I thought John and I had reached the end of our marriage." The woman sporting a chic pageboy hair style stirred a packet of sweetener into her coffee mug. The spoon made slow, almost thoughtful circles in her steaming brew. "We'd tried everything; counseling, taking vacations together away from the kids, and—" Her laugh sounded an odd mixture of rueful self-mockery and defeat, "—hypnosis."

"Hypnosis?" The second woman's eyebrows nearly disappeared beneath her heavy brown bangs.

The first woman shrugged, her lips curving into a timid grin. "I thought it'd help us fall in love again."

"And when it didn't work?"

"I called on the one person who had the answer all along: God."

Jane choked on her tea. Grabbing up a napkin and wiping her sopping chin, she couldn't help but consider the woman's reply. For the longest time, God hadn't been anything more than an expletive punctuating the end of a string of vile curses.

What made matters worse was the fact of her perfect childhood Sunday school attendance record. She'd won prizes for going faithfully every week, and for reciting the most Bible verses. Even now, she could recite Isaiah chapter fifty three. God shouldn't have been the last One on her mind. But it'd been years since she'd thought about Him.

Years since she'd prayed. Years since she'd opened her Bible. Years.

Guilt fanned the flames of turmoil in her mind. Her parents had given her the opportunity and privilege of learning about God's love and goodness, but she hadn't afforded her own children, the most precious treasures God had given her, the same blessing. Instead, she'd put them on paths leading away from the Creator of the Universe. Hearing the calm confidence in the woman's voice had hit an exposed nerve Jane hadn't been aware of.

What kind of mother was she?

Before self-recrimination started, the first woman continued speaking. "But everything changed a few months ago. My neighbor invited me to a mid-week meeting at their church, with food and fellowship at the end." She grinned and raised her hand. "Hey, anything with potluck, I'm there."

Jane's glance fell to her lap where her fingers shredded the crumpled napkin. She remembered going to meetings through the week, revival meetings when the Holy Spirit did a powerful work in each hurting heart. She needed that now more than ever but could God forgive her willful disobedience and the distance she'd put between them?

"But when the preaching started, something hit me right here." The woman pressed her open palm to her chest. "I forgot about the food. That preacher spoke candidly about an attack taking place on families today. That had me sitting up and taking it all in. It was like he was talking to me, I was the only one in that room. No one could possibly be going through the same things I was. And at the end, people were asked to stand where they were if they were on the brink of separation, divorce, or if they had a teenage rebellion on their hands.

"I held back at first, too embarrassed because I was sure I'd be the only one standing up. However, I don't think there was one person left sitting in that building." She shook her head. "And before I knew it, I was on my feet too, expecting something to happen but not sure what."

"Sounds like a typical religious experience to me," the second woman said.

"I didn't know if I'd go back, but that following Sunday morning I was there. From then on, I've discovered such comfort and joy reading my Bible and spending time alone with God in prayer. The level of intimacy I've found in Him..." She broke off as tears flooded her eyes.

Jealousy filled Jane. What the woman spoke of, she'd had the same thing a long, long time ago. And she wanted it again.

The second woman spoke with open cynicism. "Psycho babble."

"You might think that," the first woman didn't argue, but continued on gently. "Call it that if it makes you feel better, but I've experienced it for myself. All I know is that the aggravating things my husband does that made me go off like a loose cannon, I don't even react to anymore. I smile, excuse myself, and find a quiet place and discuss it with Jesus."

When the second woman didn't comment, the first continued. "Don't think my husband hasn't noticed. He has. Now he's started going to services with me." She leaned forward and said in stage whisper, "He's becoming the kind of conscientious man I never thought he'd be but always wanted. Do you know, he's not only cleaned up the supper dishes every night this week, he's even loaded the dishwasher properly?"

Jane felt her eyes widen. At her home, war was the norm, and it escalated with every chore. She'd long given up nagging her husband to take out the trash and simply did it herself, resenting him more each time.

What she wouldn't give if he even so much as took a half second to hang up his jacket when he came home from work instead of hooking it on the door knob.

Fact was, he'd been gone a week on business and the only thing she felt was relief at his absence. Even their queen size bed seemed more comfortable when she had it to herself. How long had it been since he'd indulged her with some old fashioned chocolate-and-roses romance? For that matter, a scrap of civilized conversation would be even more delicious.

As horrible as the thought was, would she care if her phone rang with the news he'd been killed in a plane crash? The stress of funeral arrangements and dealing with her children's pain would be bad, but without those factors would she really care?

The women finished their drinks and conversation and prepared to leave. Jane wished they wouldn't go, but she couldn't ask two perfect strangers to continue talking for her sake. Chewing her lower lip, she watched as they shrugged on their jackets and grabbed up their purses. She hadn't known just how starved she'd been for encouragement until she'd heard it.

However, after the first woman paid her check at the cash register, she returned to her table, tucked a five dollar tip under her plate, and then turned to Jane.

"You look like you need what I found," the woman said, pulling a square of paper from her pocket.

Jane accepted the business card with a greediness she'd have thought rude in any other social situation. But it represented a life line and 'please' and 'thank you' didn't exist in a drowning person's vocabulary.

"Hope to see you there."

Jane didn't notice when the woman left. Her attention was taken with the address of the church written in bold, red lettering. She recognized it. She had friends who attended the same congregation, friends who'd countless times invited her to go with them to various meetings.

And now two days later, she was a woman with a mission. She finished her tea, scooped her purse from the floor, paid the check, and headed back to her parked van. She'd pick up the kids from school and forego one afternoon of hockey practice in favor of visiting those same friends whose church she'd obsessed about since listening to that woman discuss the change in her life and marriage.

Jane had questions.

A lot of them.

Surely her friends would have some answers.

"Do you see them, Faith?" Half teasing, half serious, I watched my wife glance out at the busy street from the kitchen window while absently wiping a spot on the counter; the same spot she'd started cleaning ten minutes earlier.

I didn't understand her nervousness. We'd been friends with Jane, her husband and kids for three years. We'd tried talking to them about God before now, and even while they didn't seem overly eager to hear about spiritual things going on in our lives they didn't shout abuse at us either. That's why it'd been a shock when Jane unexpectedly called last night nearly begging to visit us this morning. She wanted to talk about the things she'd heard going on at our church.

"What if I say the wrong thing, Mike?" Faith finally broke her silence. I could hear panic swell in her voice as she pressed on. "What if I give a pat answer to something they're hinging all their hope on? What if I turn them off God forever? What if—"

"Honey," I braced her shoulders with my hands, "you won't."

Apparently my husbandly intuition had little effect on her. She turned towards me, narrowed her eyes and asked, "How can you be so sure?"

With a grin that oozed confidence, I simply reminded her. "We prayed about it, remember?" I massaged her tense shoulder muscles, willing her to accept the truth of what I said. "And if that's not good enough, we also enlisted twenty of the church's best prayer warriors to bring this matter to God's High Court."

"Okay, you're right." She took a deep breath, released it slowly, and flexed her fingers as she quoted. "God isn't willing for any to perish."

"Exactly." I nodded my approval, satisfied with the effect my words of encouragement had on her. It lasted as long as it took her to pick up the damp wash cloth and return to tackle the same spot on the counter.

"What?" she asked, catching my look of disappointment. "I'm doing some spiritual realm wrestling. Can I help it I get a little over eager when I pray?"

I couldn't argue with her logic. So instead, I sat down at my regular place at the dining room table, braced my elbows on my placemat and joined her in a battle invisible to human eyes.

Four eternal lives were at stake.

Caught up in a fresh anointing, I lost awareness of my surroundings. I could sense a struggle engage within my spirit. Doubt. Worry. These were enemies of the Cross. But as I silently quoted the Word, God's power filled me. I was more than a conqueror and as I remained faithful to Him, He would direct my path.

Strength renewed, my prayer ended when Faith announced that Jane's van pulled into the driveway. My smile came automatically. Three of my favorite people in the world were very soon going to have their names written in the Lamb's Book of Life, of that I had been given an Heavenly assurance.

"You probably think I'm crazy," Jane said as she and her small clan, stepped into the kitchen. "Calling you up out of the blue like that and inviting myself and the kids over."

"Not at all," my wife said with a conviction I recognized as coming from her heart. "When I told our boys you were dropping by today they went ape."

As had Faith when Jane initially told her the reason for said visit. My grin deepened. However, that piece of information I kept to myself. Instead, I called out a greeting to her and her two kids.

"I thought you were bringing the kids, Jane?" I said; my tone filled with theatrical regret. "I don't recognize these strangers."

"It's us, Uncle Mike." As one, Candace and Pete rushed at me. I stooped to receive their exuberant hugs. Candace and Pete both had Jane's blond hair and blue eyes, but they'd inherited their father's long legs.

"Well, so it is," I said, widening my eyes as if shocked. "I didn't recognize you; you've both grown so much since I last saw you."

As they roared with laughter—thinking they'd managed to fool me—my heart ached to think about the unhappiness surrounding these dear people. To an outsider, they appeared to have everything; the new cars, beautiful home, a well-paying job, and each other. However, money never solved underlying human issues. It might help, but only temporarily; pretty much the way a sling would a broken arm. The bone would heal but it'd be deformed.

This family needed the Lord to heal them as a whole unit, and individually. From personal experience, I knew the effect unkind words had on the heart. I'd hurled a few at my wife in the days before I'd surrendered my life to Christ. It took a lot of effort, apologies and reaffirmation of my love to bring about restoration between my wife and I.

And the effort had been well worth it.

"Nathan! Joel! Company!" Faith hollered to our boys, announcing Candace and Pete's presence. The house filled with whooping enthusiasm as the children greeted each other before they ran screaming through the kitchen and into the hall.

"You gotta see our fort," ten-year-old Nathan shouted out, encouraging more shouts from their guests.

"Don't break anything," Jane yelled after them before turning a sheepish grin in my direction. "Sorry about that. Hi Mike."

"Don't worry about them smashing anything," I said with a shrug. "The boys took care of breakables before they were out of diapers."

"Hard wood floors and books." Faith hit her forehead with the heel of her hand in faux seriousness. "What were we thinking?" Then she changed the subject. "Where's Brent ?"

Jane crossed her arms and lowered her gaze. "Brent is still away, but he knows I planned to be here this afternoon… and why."

"Did he mind?" Faith asked, ushering Jane into the dining room.

"I think he was relieved," Jane said, taking a seat at the table. The admission seemed to cost her something; her pride. For a half second I saw it, chunks of invisible cement with the power to anchor the soul to defeat. "We...haven't been getting along too well lately, as you know, and it seems that our final hope is God."

"That's the way it is with everyone, Jane," Faith said as she slid into the chair on my right. Her voice lacked condemnation. "It's human nature to want to do everything we possibly can in our own strength. Even when we're flat on our face chin deep in mud we still try to maintain that control."

"We usually have to get to the point of looking up at the bottom before we cry out to God for help." I put in my two cents, if only to prove that even men had the same control issues as women.

"The worse part in all of this," Jane said rubbing her arms as if chilled, "is that I once dedicated my life to God. I served

Him in church, attended services faithfully, and was involved in all the activities. The church doors were open and I was there.

"And then I met Brent." Tears filled her eyes. "I don't know what happened. My love for him eclipsed the love I felt for God. And before I knew it, I married a man who didn't know God, had no interest in God, and I built a life around him. And now my kids—" Emotion shut off her words, but the tears running down her face spoke of the state of her once bright future.

"It's too late for me." She dashed away the dampness on her face with the heel of her hand. "God probably turned His back on me like I did Him, but Candace and Pete...never stood a chance."

"Do you have breath in your lungs?" Faith asked, reaching across the table to touch Jane's wrist.

"Yes." Jane nodded, giving my wife a look that questioned her sanity.

"Then there's hope for you." Faith smiled.

"But why did I find it so easy to throw away what I had with God?"

"Because it was based on your works for God," Faith said. "Good works are good, the Bible says Christians need to be doing them, but it's not the foundation for your spiritual walk. You have to first acknowledge the price Jesus Christ paid on the cross. The shedding of His blood as a payment for your disobedience and breaking of God's law is the first step towards establishing that foundation. If you build your life on anything else but Jesus the storms of life will wash away everything you hold dear to you."

"Why didn't I get that memo before I met Brent?" Jane asked, sniffing.

"It's right there in black and white." Faith tapped her soft covered Bible beside her on the table. "But it's a lesson that we all have to learn for ourselves; one that's been going through our church, one heart at a time."

"So I've heard," Jane said, nodding. "Just like that woman at the restaurant. It's what made me call you."

"Any reason to get you to visit is all right with us, isn't it Mike?" Faith raised her gaze to me and enlisted my backup.

"You betcha." I winked at her and she smiled her gratitude.

"You and the boys and Brent are welcome here any time of the day or night." Faith patted her arm to emphasize that fact.

"Except play-offs," I said. Before my wife could frown, I held up my hands. "Just joking."

Jane laughed, the first genuine one she gave since she'd arrived at our home.

"Mike and I first heard about our church the same way you did, word of mouth," Faith said. "We felt God calling us there, and by this time our relationship had hit the dirt beneath the rocks at the bottom of the ocean."

Faith spoke the truth. Things had been bad between us. So bad we'd discussed separating. Faith would keep the house, have custody of the boys, and I'd vanish as if I'd never been a part of their lives. A lose-lose situation for our family. Praise God, He had other plans for us.

"But despite our personal problems," Faith continued, "We both wanted God to be first and foremost in our lives. However, the church didn't have a pastor at the time we started going, and it was the first assignment we took on together as a couple along with the other members of the church. I believe having that same goal is what put us back on the road to relationship recovery. Suddenly we stopped fighting as we discussed our growing enthusiasm to find the man God would put in the pulpit."

I felt the Spirit nudge me. Time for battle. Not willing to be disobedient, I picked up where Faith left off.

"You mentioned thinking it was too late, Jane," I said. "Did we ever tell you how our pastor became part of our church family?"

When Jane indicated 'no' with the shake of her head, I took a deep, steadying breath. Faith closed her eyes in prayer. We both knew these next few minutes were crucial. She'd be the Caleb to my Moses, holding up my proverbial arms in prayer.

I issued yet another silent 'thank you' to God for blessing me with a wife as wonderful and gracious as Faith, and then recounted the testimony of a man most people wouldn't have wasted garbage on.

Haden's Story

Chapter One

"Jesus loves the little children," five-year-old Haden sang with all the enthusiasm he could muster from the backseat of his dad's beat up black sedan. "All the little children of the world."

"Pipe down, kid," his father said in a tone akin to a growl. "I've got a headache."

"Maybe I should pray for you." Not discouraged, Haden rested his elbows along the back of the driver's headrest and gently rubbed his father's thinning brown hair. "Miss Nichol told me that Jesus healed a lot of people in the Bible. He might even make you stop drinking."

"Quit talking nonsense." His father jerked away from Haden's soothing fingers. "Sit back before I stop this car and plow you into next week."

Haden settled in his seat again but continued to hum the new song he'd learned in Sunday school that morning. His teacher, Miss Nichol, told all of the children in his class that Jesus had a special place in His heart for children, that it didn't matter if they were rich or poor, popular or lonely, Jesus loved them all equally. And He was always there to listen when they prayed. But most of all, He especially loved to hear His children sing songs about Him.

With complete child-like devotion, Haden trusted what Miss Nichol told him. He saw Jesus in her pretty smile, and the way her eyes lit up when she talked about Him during Sunday school. Even when she handed treats out in class, she made a point of telling them it pleased Jesus when she shared with them.

Today, Miss Nichol brought apples and bubble gum. Haden devoured his apple the moment it was in his grasp. He couldn't help it. The last meal he'd eaten had been breakfast the day before: bread with a smear of jam and half a glass of cola.

Normally he had toast in the morning, but his father hadn't paid the electric bill in nearly three months. Haden didn't know what the electric bill was beyond the fact that it meant he'd go to bed without food some nights. The pains in his stomach hurt so badly, he'd cry himself to sleep.

The treasured bubble gum remained hidden in the torn pocket in Haden's jacket. He'd save it for a special moment, like when he and his mom collected bottles along the road to buy milk and bread, enough to feed them and baby Jay.

A dark cloud passed over Haden's thoughts. Last night, his mom fell down the steps. She'd coughed nearly all night. This morning, she'd hobbled when she walked, and made squinty faces when Baby Jay kicked his feet while she held him.

"Dad," Haden picked at a peeling spot of plastic on the door, "is Mom gonna be okay?"

"Sure. She's fine."

Haden remained silent another moment before he continued. "She was breathing funny this morning."

"Listen, kid, I don't have time for any more of your stupid talk." Haden's father turned the car down a side street in an area of town that frightened Haden.

The faces of angry young men turned to stare as the car slowed down. Haden hunkered down in his seat, trying not to be seen. Music thundered from one house, all its windows were broken, and the front door hung precariously on the door frame. This was the house his father chose to park in front of.

"I'm glad our windows aren't broke," he whispered, as if to comfort himself.

"Mind your own business," His father said without turning to look at him, "and you won't get hurt."

Haden wrapped his arms around the driver side head rest and peaked around it, watching his father make his way to the front door as if he belonged there. After knocking, another man answered. They spoke for a moment before the stranger handed his father a small package. Haden didn't need to see it to know what it was. He'd seen these kinds of transactions before, and it meant strangers would come to their house at all hours of the day and night, making baby Jay cry.

He was supposed to stay in his room when that happened, but one time Haden's growing curiosity forced him to watch from the darkness of the unlit hallway. He'd seen yet another stranger pass money to Haden's father in exchange for a small parcel wrapped in cellophane.

That night his parents had another of their horrible fights. The worse one.

"You promised me you'd never do this again, Bruno!" Mom's voice choked off as she started coughing.

"Let go of my arm, Tracy." He thrust her away with his free hand. She hadn't recovered from the last time she'd fallen down the stairs, and the push sent her to the floor.

"I don't want that garbage around my babies." She glared up at him from where she struggled into a sitting position.

"This is the last time, I promise."

"You always say that." She crawled on her hands and knees to the threadbare arm chair and pulled herself to her feet. "Well, I'm sick of it. Things would be better if you were gone, or better yet, dead! You're never here when I need you, when the children need you. If you're not drunk or high, you're spending time in prison getting three square meals while we're stuck here in this hole wondering where our next bit of bread is coming from."

"You want me gone, Trac?" He bared his teeth like the wild animal he sometimes sounded like. "Fine! I'm gone."

After snatching up his grease-stained jean jacket, Haden's father slammed out of the house.

That night, Haden's nightmares woke him. He needed his mother's reassurance, her hand on her brow, to push away his fears. However, when he stood by her bed, her breathing sounded thin, as if she struggled for each breath. Her skin felt cold beneath his fingers. Though he tried to wake her, pushing at her arm, she didn't respond.

Haden didn't remember leaving the house and running to the neighbors, didn't remember when the ambulance arrived; only that his mother was gone and the grandmotherly neighbor wrapped him in a blanket and told him every thing would be okay.

It wasn't.

His father returned on the day of the funeral. Baby Jay cried through the entire ceremony but Haden didn't. He wanted to but couldn't. The tears stayed at the back of his throat and burned his eyes.

What was he going to do without his mother? Only she seemed to care what happened to him and baby Jay. Why would Jesus take her away from him? Confused, Haden wanted desperately to ask Miss Nichol why it happened. Surely, she'd know the answer.

"I'm sorry about your mother, Haden," Miss Nichol whispered to him the following Sunday morning before class. "I wish I knew why Jesus took her away from you, but I don't."

"But doesn't Jesus know I need my mom?" Haden's lower lip quivered. He hated being so weak, but something in Miss Nichol's gentle blue eyes—kindness maybe—made him feel safe.

"He does, Haden," Miss Nichol said as she wrapped her arms around him and held him close to her the way his mother used to do whenever he skinned his knee. "Jesus knows."

Haden was seated in his regular plastic chair near the door when the other children began arriving. His tears were dried now, but his face felt tight and his head ached. Miss Nichol taught about Abraham and his wife Sarah, using cut-out colored pictures to demonstrate that morning's lesson, but all the time she sent concerned glances Haden's way. The other kids noticed he was unusually quiet and kept staring at him.

After ten minutes of enduring their unspoken curiosity, Haden folded his arms on the table and hid his face. He didn't look up again until after class ended and the others were gone again.

Miss Nichol sat down on the small chair beside him and touched his shoulder. "It's going to be okay, Haden," she said.

"But I want my mom!"

"I know."

He sniffed, rubbed his nose on the sleeve of his stained shirt and stood up with a great deal of reluctance to leave her compassion-filled presence. "Dad told me this would be the last time I could go to Sunday school."

"But why?" Miss Nichol's words sounded like a yelp.

The tears clogging his throat hampered his explanation, so Haden shrugged instead.

"You know how to reach me, don't you?" Miss Nichol buttoned the top button on his filthy shirt. He'd worn it three days in a row, it smelled bad to him, but it was the cleanest shirt he had. "Anytime you need someone to talk to, you call me, okay?"

Haden nodded. He felt like he'd attended another funeral when he left the classroom that morning.

"Did you tell her?" his father asked. Haden didn't answer as he settled on the backseat of the old car with a great deal less enthusiasm than he normally showed after Sunday school.

"Well?"

Haden nodded and turned his head to the window. He'd heard his mom talk about having a heavy heart before, and now he understood because he felt like there was a cold stone in his chest where his should be beating.

"You'll thank me one day, boy." His father took the same road as the week before when he picked up the parcel. "Religion only does one thing; mess with your head."

Haden closed his eyes and leaned back in his seat. Yeah, maybe his dad was right. Even Miss Nichol, the nicest and sweetest person he knew besides his own mother, couldn't tell him why Jesus, Who loved little children, would take away the one person in the world that really cared about him.

"Nope, you stick with me kid, and one day soon we'll be on easy street." Haden's father stopped the car, rested his arm along the top of his seat and looked at Haden. "If all goes well today, we'll have money enough to last us the next twenty years."

Haden closed his eyes. He didn't care about money.

Chapter Two

"Keep the doors locked while I'm out, kid," Haden's father said. He took one last look at his reflection in the grime-streaked mirror in the hall and passed a comb through his ever thinning dark hair. Hair that now reflected grey in the bald light dangling from the ceiling.

"Where you goin'?" eight year old Haden asked, but he knew the answer already. Saturdays were always the same in their home; Bruno would spend the day passed out on the sofa after visiting the local bar Friday night, and then Saturday evening he'd head out to the same place.

"None of your business," Bruno said striding for the front door. His words more a snap than the usual snarl this time. "Don't let anyone in while I'm gone."

"Yes, sir."

What Bruno really meant was don't let the neighbors know about the stash of drug money hidden under the floor board in the coat closet. And most definitely don't mention the names of people Bruno associated with. Never know when an undercover police officer might show up acting like a druggie with the intent of capturing a prime piece of heroine-pushing garbage like Bruno.

"Wish me luck, kid," Bruno paused by the door and sent his son a grin. "Tonight might be the night we strike it rich. And then I can get us a real place away from the rats and stink of this place."

"Luck," Haden said, biting his lower lip. He'd given up hoping for better a long time ago. With Bruno, the next gig was going to be the get-rich-quick one, and always his hopes were in vain.

The door slammed shut and moments later the sound of the old sedan's stuttering engine faded into the night.

Sighing with relief at finally being alone, Haden turned his attention to the radio left on in the living room. The television had been sold a long time ago to pay off one of Bruno's cohorts. He'd never owned a gaming system, couldn't read very well, and he wasn't allowed outside to play, in case someone forced information about Bruno out of him. But what he did enjoy was listening to live broadcasts of hockey games.

Tonight Montreal played against Edmonton. Haden rooted for the Oilers.

Without a cursory thought to the state of cleanliness of the mud-stained carpet, Haden stretched out on the floor and listened to the announcers give a play-by-play of the game.

This was the only time he didn't ache for his mother or his baby brother. When his mother died, Jay had been snatched up by their aunt and uncle. They'd always wanted a baby, but not a half grown child with a dirty face and the potential to eat his weight in groceries.

At first, the nights he'd been left alone in the house had been the loneliest ones he'd ever known. Once, he tried to talk to Jesus but then he remembered his mother's death and anger and sorrow silenced him. After that, he stopped praying to Someone that probably never existed.

How could a God who really cared take away everyone he'd ever loved and leave him with the person who didn't care if he lived or died. Bruno didn't care if he didn't eat for days at a time, didn't concern himself about the state of Haden's clothes, and especially didn't care if his son had no one to love.

After a time, the anger changed to something more elemental, more destructive.

Hatred.

The hockey game was nearly over when the slam of the back door shook Haden out of his comfortable, half-doze.

"Dad?"

"I was here all night," Bruno said as he shook out of his heavy black coat and tossed it on the floor of the coat closet. Despite it being a cold, dry night, his hair looked damp.

"What—"

"If anyone comes to that door," Bruno talked over him, "I was with you right here listening to the game." Then he turned and stomped down the hallway. Haden, unable to contain his growing anxiety over his father's odd behavior, followed him.

"Dad?"

Haden found his father in the bathroom. Bruno didn't pause from where he stood over the bathroom sink washing his hands and his blood-crusted knuckles. Haden's gaze traveled up to his father's face, seeing it for the first time since he'd returned home. What he saw evoked a gasp.

Blood oozed from cuts on his forehead and cheeks. The skin around his eyes were swelling and turning blue and purple.

"What happened?" Haden asked, running to the linen closet and pulling out a tattered brown towel. Bruno took it from him and dabbed with a great deal of caution at his cuts, grunting when he moved on to a new spot.

"Had an accident," he snapped. "Get me the peroxide."

"With the car?" Haden found a bottle of peroxide on the same shelf as the haphazardly folded towels.

"Yeah, the car." Bruno grabbed the bottle and doused the towel with clear liquid, "What are you, stupid or something?"

Haden stepped back, wary of his father in his agitated state. In this mood, Haden never knew when he'd launch a backhand in his direction.

"Are...are you okay?"

"Do I look okay?" Bruno pressed a corner of the wet towel to his cuts. "The car's a write off."

The door bell rang. They both froze.

"It's the cops." Bruno took another look at his reflection before tossing the towel aside. "Remember, I been here all night. Get me a beer, dump half in the sink."

Without another question, Haden did as told. Whatever was going on, it had to be bad if his father permitted a drop of his precious alcohol poured down the drain.

"Go sit down," Bruno commanded after Haden handed him the beer can. Haden returned to the living room while his father went to answer the front door.

The game was over now, Montreal won. Haden sat down in the armchair and chewed his lower lip, anticipating something bad but not sure what exactly.

He heard another male voice but not what was being said. With curiosity and a sense of impending doom, Haden tiptoed to a vantage spot to overhear the conversation.

"Sorry, officer, been here all night. Ask the kid."

"Then how did your car get down town?"

"Did you look at this place? Cars are stolen every day."

"I don't have a report of yours being stolen."

"Then someone at head quarters didn't do their job."

"Mr. Lambert, the point is, a family of three were killed tonight when your car ran a red light and smashed into their van."

"I'm sorry to hear that."

The only sounds that followed that statement were silence and the odd hitch in Bruno's breathing.

"Let me talk to your boy, Mr. Lambert."

"Haden!"

Panicked at the idea of facing the police officer, Haden didn't move.

"Haden!" The warning in his father's voice was unmistakable.

After taking a deep breath, Haden moved away from the corner of the wall and stepped into the lighted hall. He hunched his shoulders and didn't look anywhere other than at his feet.

"Yeah, Dad?"

"Tell this nice officer where I've been all evening."

"Here. We were listening to the hockey game on the radio."

"Who won?" the officer asked.

"Montreal," Haden answered automatically.

"Good for them." The police officer nodded, and then redirected his gaze to Bruno. "Okay, I'll check on the stolen car report, make sure it was filed. Don't make any plans to leave the city for a while."

"Thank you, officer." Bruno opened the door for the other man, as if politeness and not beer ran in his blood. Haden scowled at his father, despising the older man for being a con artist, liar, and a drug dealer.

Bruno maintained his innocent smile until the officer left the house and the door was firmly closed behind his back. Then panic broke out.

"I ain't going to jail again," Bruno said heading into the living room. "That's what'll happen when they find out I'd lied about the car being stolen. And my life won't be worth spit when the guys hear I left the drugs in the car when I split after the accident. I got to get out of here."

Fear distorted Haden's common sense. He'd seen his father in these moods before and knew better than to get in the way, but the idea of being left completely alone terrified him. He'd heard the stories of social services taking kids away and dumping them in foster care with strangers; strangers who did bad things.

"What about me?" Haden asked, following his father.

"What about you?" Bruno looked about the room, as if searching for something.

"Who's going to look after me?"

"That's not my problem now, kid." Bruno sneered. "Look after yourself. I did it when I was your age." He pounced on the arm chair cushion, tossing it aside to reveal a gun. "You got any money?"

Haden gaped at the foreign idea. "No."

"I must have some around here somewhere."

"What about the drug money?" Haden suggested.

"Are you crazy? I touch that and I'm dead."

When the door bell rang again, Haden stopped breathing.

"Check and see who that is." Bruno jerked his head towards the door.

Haden did as he was told. After a quick peek, he said, "It's Eon."

He'd recognized the man from Bruno's gang, the guy they sent in to clean up messes when mistakes were made by their members. If things hadn't been bad before, Eon tripled their problems.

"They know!" Bruno went into a frenzy. Gun in hand, he ran down the hall into the kitchen. This time Eon pounded on the door.

Haden backed into the living room, as if trying to avoid a rabid dog. In essence, that's exactly what Eon reminded Haden of; an animal driven wild by his lust for blood.

The sound of the locked door knob jiggling sped up Haden's heart. He didn't doubt they were going to die.

Finally losing patience, Eon raised his booted foot and kicked into the glass in the door, reached into the gaping opening and unlocked the door.

"Where's your dad?"

Haden stared up at the tall man who looked like he spent most of his free time at the gym. Despite the chill in the night air, Eon was sleeveless, showing off his steroid-induced muscles. The military cut of his hair coupled with the smooth fierce scowl on his face earned the man immediate respect. The ugly silver handgun in his hand more so.

"Uh…" The ability to speak failed Haden in the face of his living nightmare.

"Stupid kid," Eon muttered. "I'll find him myself."

As if wearing a honing device, Eon bee-lined for the kitchen.

"You made your last mistake, Lambert," Eon said conversationally.

"Give me another chance," Bruno begged.

Haden pictured his father begging for the mercy he'd never willingly give anyone else; not his wife, and not his own kids. He squeezed his eyes shut in anticipation of what was to come.

However, it didn't matter that he'd braced for it, the sound of a single gun shot jerked him off his feet. Haden clasped the arm of the sofa and waited for Eon to find him. If he'd thought running would help, he'd have ducked for cover, but no one ever got away when Eon decided they needed to die.

Slow, heavy footfalls sounded in the hall a moment later. In that moment, Haden relived his last moments of Sunday school while waiting to die. It'd been years since he'd thought of Miss Nichols but oddly enough her face came before his closed eyes with perfect clarity.

She'd feel bad when she'd heard about his death. No matter what his father said, she'd cared. He shouldn't have stopped going to Sunday school, even if he'd had to sneak away to go.

"You can stop cringing, kid." Eon's loud voice pierced the heavy silence in the house. "I'm going to let you live. But remember this; don't mess with my gang. If you do, you won't get another chance."

Haden didn't open his eyes for what felt like hours. His legs shook as he made his way to the kitchen. Fear and morbid curiosity forced him into the room where his father had tried to escape his gang's justice.

Haden spotted his father laying face down on the kitchen table; blood pooled around his head. He didn't remembered calling the police, but they seemed to appear as if by magic, pushing him to the side while they examined the crime scene. Lead weights filled his stomach as he watched the way his father was zipped into a body bag and rolled out of the house on a stretcher.

"You'll be alright, Haden," the old woman who lived next door tried to comfort him with warm reassurances, but they didn't reach his stone cold heart. Everyone was gone, and he only had himself to depend on.

Chapter Three

Haden lay on the floor, face down as the sounds of heavy footsteps receded down the stairs. Ragged, shallow breaths fluttered in his lungs.

He hurt, as if every bone in his underfed frame had been crushed beneath a giant shoe. Death couldn't be worse than this, he thought, pushing up into a kneeling position. Death would take him away from his uncle's sick violence. Death would bring peace.

Four years. Had it really been that long since Eon had killed his father? Would Bruno have cared if he'd known Haden would end up living with a man who took great pleasure in beating and doing other nameless horrors to a child?

No. The answer resonated in Haden's mind. In his lifetime, never once had his father given a moment's consideration to how his actions affected the rest of his family. He never cared if they didn't have food in the house, the bills paid, or if they'd have a roof over their heads. All that mattered to Bruno Lambert was scoring his next big drug haul or burglarizing the homes of decent, hardworking people.

Grinding his teeth, Haden hobbled to the shabby dresser in the corner of his small bedroom with the intent of getting his few articles of clothing together. Never again, he vowed. Never again would anyone hurt him like this.

The night air worked its magic on Haden, clearing his head as he reached through the open window until he grabbed hold of the branches of the maple tree near the house. His left foot found purchase on the tree and within moments he descended using branches as rungs. He picked up the backpack of clothes he'd dropped out the window earlier, gingerly shouldered it, and made his way to the road taking care to stay in the shadows in case his uncle happened to notice him from the house.

This was what freedom felt like, Haden grimaced. No one to care where he went, no money in his pockets, and no home to call his own. At least he didn't have to endure any more of his uncle's violence. That thought alone added a pound of determination to his already overflowing cache of resolve to make his own way in the world.

Perhaps he'd find out where his brother lived, and maybe his relatives would take pity on him. However, Haden prepared for the worse. He'd had to in order to survive the past few years since his mother died. No one took his problems into consideration and showed him pity.

This was the real world. He sniffed, rubbing away the tears that ran down his face with his fisted hands. This was the way to become master of his own destination. No one would ever take his choices away from him.

And no one would ever make him cry again.

Three days later, while scavenging for food in a dumpster outside the local diner, a police officer approached Haden before he had a chance to vanish into the shadows.

"What are you doing, Son?"

"Nothing." Haden took a slow, sly step back.

"Shouldn't you be home? It's pretty late for you to be out and about now."

"My folks don't mind."

"Why don't you tell me who your parents are and where you live?"

"No!" Haden backed up another step, preparing to run. "I didn't break any law."

"Never said you did, Son." The police officer advanced.

Like a wild animal cornered, Haden lunged at the officer, counting on the element of surprise to get away. It'd worked before when other strangers had approached him. However, the officer figured out what he was up to. He easily trapped Haden under his arm.

"Easy, Son. I just want to talk to you."

"I got nothing to say." Haden lashed out with his booted foot but didn't manage to connect with the officer's shin.

"Your parents must be worried sick about you."

"They're dead." Haden continued squirming, but no matter what he did the officer held on. However, days of going without more than a handful of rotting sandwiches he'd found in the dumpster and mouthfuls of rain water caught up with him. With a groan of exhaustion, Haden collapsed. He would have fallen if the officer didn't have a grip on the back of his tattered jacket.

"Where were you living before coming out here?"

"With my uncle, but he hurt me real bad. Please don't make me go back."

"If what you say is true there's no way you're going back there. I'll make sure of it," the officer assured him. "But right now it looks like you could use a good meal, a bath, and a nice warm bed to sleep in."

It sounded good to Haden but he didn't let the officer know just how much. Weakness meant giving someone an edge over you. The thought of more abuse knotted Haden's empty stomach.

Within the hour, the officer found a comfortable place for Haden with nice people. They were his first contact with the foster care system. However, instead of being grateful for the comfortable bed, the clean sheets, and the best tasting food he'd ever shoveled into his greedy mouth, Haden remained aloof. Their overtures of friendship went ignored.

The child welfare system left Haden with the kind couple, and enrolled him in the local school.

He didn't fit in with the kids at his new school. His propensity to bully younger children earned him the nickname Hades. After a couple months of complaints from the teachers, his foster parents decided he was too much for them to handle.

The next home Haden moved to wasn't quite as nice. And it didn't take long to figure out they only wanted him there because of the money the system shelled out for his upkeep. Not that he saw much of that. If he received a new pair of jeans and shirt he was lucky. And meals were quick, easy, and cheap; macaroni being the main staple.

"Why you so mean, Hades?" His best friend, Trevor, asked him one day while reading a comic book and eating candy at the convenience store. "It's like you got a big chip on your shoulder, like my foster dad tells me I got all the time."

"I dunno." Haden shrugged, but he knew why. The image of his dead father continued to haunt him. No matter how hard he tried to convince himself he didn't care, the pain of rejection dogged his every waking moment. And then there were the nightmares of what his uncle had put him through.

After being shooed out of the store for loitering, the boys sat on their stolen bicycles eating chocolate bars.

"Well, whatever it is that's bugging you," Trevor said, "my friend, Buddy can fix you up with something that'll make the world a whole lot easier to deal with."

"Sounds good," Haden said. He suspected Trevor meant drugs. And he wasn't disappointed when Buddy later showed him a sample of his drug paraphernalia.

"I recommend this to all my new customers," Trevor's friend said, pulling a clear bag of what looked like some kind of spice from his shirt pocket.

"How much it cost?" Trevor asked.

"Well, seeing as it's your first time," the taller boy said, eyeing Haden much like an art dealer might a painting. "You can have this for free. But the next time, it'll cost you."

"Thanks, man," Trevor said, taking the bag and shoving it at Haden. "We'll be back."

"I know you will." Buddy gave a harsh laugh before leaving them alone in the alley.

"You up for this stuff, Hades?"

"I guess."

"You're in for a real treat. Buddy's stuff is the best."

Haden forgot what it felt like not to care about anything. In fact, he relaxed as Trevor showed him how to roll a cigarette and light it. They took turns smoking the joint, and Haden like the feeling it gave him. But like everything else, the feeling didn't last and he needed another fix.

"I don't have that money," Haden said, shocked at the amount Buddy quoted for a bag of marijuana.

"S'up to you," Buddy said, turning away. "I got other customers who're willing to pay for this stuff."

"No, wait!" Haden gritted his teeth when Buddy looked at him expectantly. "I can get it."

"Sorry, no credit."

"I said I'll get it."

"And you'll know where to find me when you do."

The problem was Haden didn't know where he'd get money. But his desperation for the drug drove him to scheme. When he mentioned his dilemma to Trevor, his friend had yet another answer to his problem.

"I been meaning to ask you this before," Trevor said, turning the page of his comic book. "You can make some quick cash delivering packages for some people I know."

"What's in them?"

"Dunno. Never asked. All I know is they pay good and on time. Interested?"

"Yeah."

"I'll ask around and get back to you."

"Make it soon, will ya?" Haden wiped his damp brow with the back of his hand. His experience with marijuana left him with a never ending longing for more.

"Count on it." Trevor chuckled before tossing the comic book to Haden. "Come on. I'll show you the place."

The boys biked downtown to a non-descript apartment building. While Haden waited, Trevor strutted up the concrete steps with an arrogance that Haden secretly admired. His friend didn't seem to be afraid of anyone or anything. Haden wish he felt the same way, but fear followed hard on his heels no matter where he turned.

Chapter Four

[Ten Years Later]

Haden stood at the bathroom sink, shaving the bristly shadow from his jaw line when the phone rang next to his king-sized bed. After tapping the excess shaving cream and whiskers from the razor, he answered it on the fourth ring.

"I got another contact for you." Trevor's voice came over the line. "They have the best merchandise this side of Columbia." In the years they'd been friends, Trevor was the one mainstay in Haden's life. And the one person Haden trusted above all others. "I also cut the competition's legs out from under him."

"Good," Haden said, rubbing his chin with one end of the towel draped over his shoulders. "They were breathing down my neck a little too often for my liking."

"I'm sure there will be more," Trevor said with the hint of a sigh in his liquor-ravaged voice. "You know what young punks are like nowadays."

"Yeah, know it all too well." Haden agreed, thinking of a couple times when he'd had to put a few pushy kids in their place.

"Listen, Hades, that's not the reason I called," Trevor said, switching gears. "I'm in Vegas right now. Word is someone's hired a gun to take you out. This guy's deadly. Only way to end it is to get him first."

"That's nothing new." Haden closed his eyes as weariness seeped into his bones. When was the last time he'd had a good night's sleep, he wondered.

"Does the name Eon ring a bell?"

Haden's eyes flared open.

"What do you know about him?" Haden asked, careful to keep his tone level. Even friends didn't need to know when you were feeling nervous; particularly friends in this type of work.

"Old as Methuselah, but deadly." Trevor went down the list of the hired killer's credentials. "He's in top shape; it's what kept him alive all these years. Shows his targets no mercy, and needs only one bullet to seal a deal."

Yep, same Eon.

"You still there?" Trevor asked when Haden didn't reply.

"Sometimes I wonder if this life is worth all the hassle," Haden said, taking a glance around his room.

Things had turned around for him since he'd struck up a friendship with Trevor. Finding employment moving parcels for people had brought in the kind of money that quickly established his career with the mob. The irony was that he'd achieved exactly what his father had wanted. Haden had the cars, the houses, the jewelry, but at what price? He had no one to share them with.

Shrugging off the depressing thoughts, Haden concentrated on what was most important right now: preserving his own life.

"Oh, yeah, it's worth it, man," Trevor was quick to assure him. "You're getting soft if you don't remember being kicked around from foster home to foster home, eating out of garbage bins, and feeling less than human."

"Okay, you're right. Lost my head for a minute." Haden tossed the towel around his neck to the floor. Housekeeping would get it when they cleaned his room.

"Good, now listen up. I'll tell you what I heard about this guy."

Haden hung up the phone a few minutes later after Trevor gave him details about the lies being spread about him and the person hired to kill him. Eon.

Blowing out a breath, he quickly plotted the details that would get him to Las Vegas, and take out his father's killer. He remembered the warning Eon had given him those years ago, about not messing with his gang. But that was then and Haden wasn't a scared kid anymore.

In fact, this wouldn't be the first time Haden killed someone. He'd gained the admiration of many of his mob friends with his aptitude with everything from knives to semi-automatics. First, he'd had to get clean from his drug addiction to make it as far in the mob as he had. The people he'd killed were the kind of low-life's no one would miss: especially the pedophiles.

His anger gave him an edge a lot of other people didn't have. It made him dangerous and unpredictable. But no one had ever questioned his reputation before. Having a rival gang take out a contract on someone wasn't new. Haden knew he was that good that this contract didn't surprise him.

Las Vegas was one of Haden's least favorite places in the world. The glitter, the hype, the relentless energy; it was exhausting. And ironically it was his bread and butter.

He checked into his favorite low-profile motel, settled into the small, dingy room, and called Trevor. His friend gave him Eon's address.

Haden focused a lifetime of anger on getting rid of the reason why he'd ended up in his uncle's home in the first place. Eon would suffer before being snuffed out like the diseased beast he was.

However, before making any hasty moves, Haden decided to get a good night sleep. With Eon gone, his reputation as a ruthless killer would skyrocket and no one would make any more attempts on his life. For a while.

No more than two hours passed when someone pounded on the door. As always, Haden's memory shot back to the night the police officer came to their door when he was a kid; the night Eon killed his father.

"Hold on," he shouted when the pounding started again.

When he opened the door it was as if he morphed back into that scared kid. It didn't matter that he'd grown from a fifty pound half starved waif into six feet of solid muscle and tattoos. The sight of the uniformed officers standing just outside his motel door twisted his stomach into knots. Swallowing hard, he somehow found the strength to act semi-normal. After all, there wasn't anything they could pin on him. He hadn't done anything illegal in Vegas. Yet.

"Are you Haden Lambert?"

"Yes." It'd been years since Haden had been referred to as anything else but Hades. His guts quivered like jelly in the hot sun.

"I have a warrant for your arrest. You have the right to remain silent. Anything-"

"What's this all about?" Haden demanded as the officer's partner cuffed him.

"Murder."

"What? I didn't kill nobody. I just got to Vegas this evening."

"If you don't have a lawyer, one will be provided." The first officer continued reading Haden his rights as if he hadn't interrupted.

He'd been through the system enough times to know it wouldn't help to protest, so he remained compliant as they led him away to the police car, it's lights flashing where it was parked in the lot next to his rental car. Haden glared at the curious expressions on the faces peaking through curtains in the other motel rooms until the second officer put a hand on his head and pushed him into the back seat of the car.

The holding cell at the police station was windowless, barred, and claustrophobic. Haden sat down on the only empty space on the bench and breathed through his mouth. Putrid odors weren't new to him, especially unwashed flesh and urine, but since making the kind of money that kept him in luxury he hadn't felt the bite of poverty.

But this was a new level of low.

"What you in for?" one of the older gentlemen directed the slurred question to Haden. His rumpled clothes and stink of liquor gave him away as a drunkard.

"Being anti-social." Haden coughed and stood up. He didn't turn his back on the men in the cage with him. One never knew why they were there, and he didn't want to take a chance they were nothing more dangerous than jaywalkers.

Haden didn't close his eyes the rest of the night. Not that he could have slept. Close quarters with low life garbage didn't necessitate friendly confidences.

It was nearly noon the next day before Haden was told exactly why he was there.

"You killed Bill Cane, aka Eon." An officer leaned across the scarred table in the small room where they questioned him.

"No, sir." Haden shook his head, crossing his arms over his chest. They could say anything and he was determined not to react.

"We have a taped conversation between you and your friend, Trevor Gaines," another officer said.

"That don't prove a thing." Haden felt his grip on his anger slipping. He always checked his phone for bugs. The only way they overheard anything was through Trevor. A tremor of betrayal raced down his spine. If he'd been sold out—

"We'll see what the judge thinks at your hearing."

Two months later, prosecution had done their research and the verdict came down. Haden was found guilty of one count of first degree murder, drug trafficking, and illegal money laundering. It earned him thirty years in maximum security with the possibility of parole.

Things couldn't have been worse.

Chapter Five

All his life, Haden heard about prison. His father lived that life. He never expected to follow in his father's footsteps, but circumstances had a way of setting your foot down a path you despise.

For him, that path led to the single cell. Gone was his privacy, luxury, and freedom. A metal, secured-to-the-wall cot and toilet were all the luxuries afforded Haden now. As the door slammed behind his prison uniformed back, Haden glanced around him, disoriented. So this was what it felt like to lose all sense of self.

From his father's stories, he knew he'd have one hour of exercise in the yard—a highly secured area where the inmates played basketball, sat around and talked, and got fresh air and sunshine. It also meant socializing with some of the state's most dangerous criminals. That being the case, he'd have to find a place with men of his own color. Not that he was racial, but that's how the system worked.

You stayed with your own 'kind' to stay alive.

Within a couple days, Haden found a group of guys of his own ilk, and remained closed mouth over his situation, the reason he was there, and his background. Showing signs of weakness at the beginning would be like slitting his wrist in shark-infested waters. And these convicted murderers, rapists, and drug pushers had the deadliest teeth in the ocean.

Besides, it wouldn't take long for someone to find out the reason why he was serving thirty years. Information always made its way into the general prison population in no time.

What Haden didn't expect was respect from the other guys. His reputation had followed on his heels into prison, and within a short time, he was operating another highly successful drug ring inside the prison, and dealing in non-contraband items like toilet paper and candy.

It also didn't take long to become a threat to king pins from gang rivals. Haden didn't care. What was his life worth anyway?

"You're worth more than you realize, Haden," Bob, the prison chaplain, told him one day in his office.

"My father didn't think so." Haden crossed his arms over his chest and stared at the barred window above the Chaplain's head. The only reason he met with the chaplain every week was to make it look like he might be reforming, therefore making him a candidate for early parole.

"Your father bought into a lie." Chaplain Bob shifted in his seat, leaning forward and holding out the black covered Bible in his left hand. "But the truth, it always brings freedom."

"I don't believe in God," Haden snarled. "I don't believe there's a devil. I believe in me and what I can do with my own hands."

"And what about eternity, Haden? Where will you spend it?"

Haden stared at the Chaplain for a long moment. If he didn't think the other man truly cared, he might have punched him out for his religious fanaticism. But as it was, the chaplain had proven countless times that he cared; times when he'd put his own needs before others. Many winter nights he'd been called away from his warm bed to council one of the prisoners who needed comfort. Lots of times he'd went to bat for a prisoner when they faced an injustice at the hands of a prison guard.

"If there is a Hell," Haden said, "and I don't think there is, then I'll be partying with my buddies."

"Time's up, Lambert." The guard opened the door and made the announcement with a smug grin. Unlike Bob, they weren't fooled by his sudden interest in religious instruction.

"Pencil me in for next week, Chaplain," Haden said, "I'm sure I'll have other questions for you. In fact, I'd like to get your take on why my mother died and left me to deal with a conscienceless father and then a sadistic pervert."

"You have a standing invitation," the chaplain said kindly as he wrote down Haden's next appointment in his day planner.

Haden, his wrists cuffed, left the office grinning. It was so easy to sucker Bible Thumpers. Their bleeding hearts made them prime victims. And while he sneered at the chaplain's mercy he also appreciated it, but he'd never admit that.

Haden barely had time to think about what the chaplain had told him that day. For weeks, tensions were building between rival gangs, Haden's included, and on his way back to his cell the rage spilled over.

A riot broke out among the prisoners. Men were fighting in packs, blacks and whites lunging at each other's throats. Hand-made knives flashed with deadly intent in the artificial light.

Pressing against the cold wall, Haden realized the vulnerability of his position. His guard escort had disappeared the moment the riot began, forgetting to release Haden from the cuffs.

The safest place he could have been was his in cell. In the open, he was a sitting duck. And it didn't go unnoticed.

"Hades!"

His head turned, and he immediately broke into a sweat at the man stalking his way. Break House, a member of his own gang, had proved over time to be his most dangerous rival. Haden's gaze slid down to the makeshift blade in Break House's hand.

"I'm gonna enjoy roasting your kidneys in the yard," Break House said, advancing on him.

Haden crouched, ready to use his feet in self-defense. However, his hopes of survival decreased significantly when Break House's buddy appeared behind Haden's right shoulder.

"Boo!" Jonestown whispered in his ear, raising his own crude knife.

The attack was over in less than a minute. Haden slid down the cement wall, leaving streaks of blood on its cold surface. Life dimmed in his eyes, until they closed in darkness.

"Help me!" Haden gasped, hauling air into his lungs as if he'd run a marathon. "Help me," he screamed, jackknifing into a sitting position. "God! Help me!"

"Easy, Haden," a kind, familiar voice spoke with calm assurance. "You're in the infirmary."

"I saw it, Chaplain!" Haden struggled beneath the hospital sheet but didn't have the strength. "I saw Hell."

Even now he could smell the sulfur, hear the screams of souls in agony. The experience held him in an icy fist. The shaking started at his toes and enveloped him.

"You were in a coma for three days," the chaplain said, putting his arms around Haden's quaking shoulders. The doctors didn't think you'd make it. We were praying God would have mercy on you, Haden."

Another time, Haden would have shook off the comfort and sneered, but what he'd just experienced, he'd take any lifeline offered. Even the small Bible in the chaplain's shirt pocket offered hope in his otherwise hopeless life.

No way did he want to go through what he'd just seen. Especially if Hell was for keeps.

"Read something to me out of your book, Chaplain," he begged. "Something that tells me I got hope. That I haven't crossed a line and God isn't gonna give up on me."

The chaplain reached for the pocket Bible and found hope for Haden in black and white.

"And as Moses lifted up the serpent in the wilderness, even so must the Son of man be lifted up;

"That whosoever believeth in him should not perish, but have eternal life.

"For God so loved the world, that he gave his only begotten Son, that whosoever believeth in him should not perish, but have everlasting life.

"For God sent not his Son into the world to condemn the world; but that the world through him might be saved.

"He that believeth on him is not condemned: but he that believeth not is condemned already, because he hath not believed in the name of the only begotten Son of God.

"And this is the condemnation, that light is come into the world, and men loved darkness rather than light, because their deeds were evil.

"For every one that doeth evil hateth the light, neither cometh to the light, lest his deeds should be reproved.

"But he that doeth truth cometh to the light, that his deeds may be made manifest, that they are wrought in God."

Hugging his body with his arms, recognition flared in Haden's memory of a time he thought he'd forgotten. "That's from the book of John, isn't it?" His teeth chattered, but he managed to make himself understood.

"Why—yes it is." To say the chaplain was surprised was an understatement. His eyes bulged and his mouth hung open at the idea that one of the prison's most anti-religious inmates was familiar with a Bible verse. "How did you know?"

"I used to go to Sunday school as a kid. Miss Nichols, my teacher, led us kids in a prayer one morning. I asked Jesus into my heart…but then I turned my back on Him." His head lowered, defeated. "He won't forgive me for walking away now."

"We just read about that," The chaplain reminded him. "If you're sincere in your desire to follow Him, to forsake your evil ways, then yes, Jesus will forgive you."

Two weeks later, when Haden had a chance to gain his strength back from the attack, he was transferred to another maximum security prison.

Chapter Six

"Are you Haden?"

Lowering the Bible in his hands, Haden glanced up from where he rested on his cot. Through the bars, he saw a slight man wearing a tag identifying him as the prison chaplain.

"Yeah." The pain from his stab wound had faded, and time was healing the injury, but he still needed recovery time.

"I'm Pastor Blair. A friend of yours from the other prison thought I should know about you. I figured I'd introduce myself and invite you to the church service we're having tonight. Mike Newman is speaking."

Haden never heard of Mike Newman but he was interested. The experience he'd had, that horrifying vision of Hell, while in the coma left him with the desperation to live for Christ.

Before he'd left the other prison, his friend, Bob, had given him a pocket Bible, much like the one the chaplain carried with him at all times. He devoured the words on the pages, and at one point had echoed the cry of the tax collector's prayer; "God be merciful to me a sinner."

"Nothing could stop me from going," Haden said in reference to the meeting, and meant it. If anyone from his former life could see him now, they wouldn't believe that a man with his depth of hatred, anger, and moral decay could be the same one believing in a God he'd once denied existed.

Who said God didn't have a sense of humor?

That evening, a guard escorted Haden to the common room where chairs were set up facing a plain wooden podium. A handful of other men in prison attire already sat in a few of the plastic orange chairs. Haden and most of the others carried Bibles.

"Welcome, Haden," Chaplain Blair greeted him at the door with a firm handshake. "So glad you're here."

"Wouldn't miss this for anything, Pastor," Haden said. "There's a Hell I want to shun and a Heaven to gain."

"Those are wise words." Pastor Blair smiled with approval. "Please, have a seat."

Despite surrendering his life to God, not all his habits had disappeared; Haden realized as he chose a seat in the back row. Given the kind of people he was forced to socialize with every day, he didn't feel comfortable leaving his back vulnerable to strangers, even if this was a church service.

Moments later, Pastor Blair made his way to the podium and welcomed every one in attendance before opening the meeting with prayer. Then he gave a brief introduction for Mike Newman, a traveling speaker, with a heart for prisoners.

The big man stood up, Bible in hand, and headed for the podium. Wearing jeans and a plaid shirt, Mike Newman could have been any man. However, when he opened his mouth and gave his testimony, Haden realized he was in the presence of one of God's emissaries.

"It was nothing for me to steal from my own family," Mike Newman said. "My children had toys, and I'd sell them for drugs. Nothing was off limits if it meant I'd get that next high.

"But then I met the One who gave me the greatest high. His name is Jesus Christ. And if you've never met Him, let me introduce you. He's the Savior of the world, the One who died on a cross for everyone's sins, beaten, bloodied, had a crown of thorns pushed into His skull." He glanced around the room. "I see a few of you men have beards. So did Jesus, and His was ripped out of His face."

A handful of men cringed at the thought.

Haden couldn't begin to imagine the pain the Son of God endured for his sake. Guilt pressed down on his shoulders and he hung his head as Mike Newman's words continued; relentless, heartbreaking, and to the point.

"A sword was thrust into his side by a burly soldier, and blood and water poured out of Him. While His own mother looked on and watched the child she'd given birth to going through this abuse, Jesus, the one Who this world mocks, in all His agony, still made sure His earth mother was looked after before He died on that cross.

"We think we have it rough when someone cuts in the lunch line ahead of us, or when things don't go the way we think it should. But I tell you now, this is nothing compared to what Jesus Himself went through—not because He deserved to die, but because we do, and yet in His mercy and love and grace, while we were yet sinners, He died for us. Friend, don't turn down what His sacrifice paid for. Don't believe the lies of the enemy, lies that say you can't make things right with the One Who died for you. He's waiting for you."

Haden's shoulders shook as sobs wrenched his soul. It was one thing to have an experience with Hell, it was another to see the price paid by the One Who cared enough to die to make sure a filthy drug dealer like he'd been, Hades Lambert, had access to the way out.

"I'm sorry, Jesus." He moaned against his clenched fist. "I'm sorry."

And in that common room, head and heart bowed before his Savior, Haden became a new man.

"This is just the beginning, Haden," Pastor Blair told him after the service when most of the prisoners had left the common room. A guard waited in the corner for Haden but didn't seem to be in a hurry, leaving Haden a chance to speak privately with the pastor. "You're going to find your attitude and thoughts will be completely different because of what Christ is doing in you."

"I'm glad," Haden said with a shuddering breath. "I couldn't stand the thoughts going through my head anymore."

"Those thoughts were inspired by Hell, and it no longer has any hold on you, my friend." Pastor Blair dropped his hand on Haden's shoulder and squeezed. "Welcome home."

For the next few years, Haden kept Pastor Blair busy with questions about the Bible, and God's will for him. Each question was met with scriptures and the two men prayed together, often praying through Haden's tough situations. Under Pastor Blair's guidance and mentoring, Haden grew spiritually and became a model prisoner. His testimony spread among the men. There were those who sneered and mocked him for his Christian stand but others admired him for his determination and the changes God had made in his life.

"I need to speak with you, Haden," Pastor Blair said one morning after Sunday service in the common room. "How would you like to work in my office?"

"That'd be great!" It meant the two men could talk and pray more often, something Haden looked forward to all week. "I'm definitely interested."

"I've already spoken to the prison warden, and because of your exemplary behavior over the course of the past three years he feels you deserve this opportunity."

Haden waited until he returned to his cell before he gave tearful thanks and praise to God for the miracle of being able to spend more time with the pastor, and being mentored.

For the next two years Haden was saturated with prayer, Bible study, and conversation with God. God spoke to him in dreams and visions and scriptures. They were the best days of Haden's life. He didn't think they'd get any better, but God had another surprise for him.

"How long have we known each other, Haden?" Pastor Blair asked him one day while they drank coffee and read the Bible together. "Five and a half years now?"

"About that." Haden nodded, half listening to the question as he continued reading the book of Job in silence.

"You've come a long way. Not only do you work in the office here, but you've completed a correspondent pastoral course. You counsel the men in your block, and have gained the trust of the guards and warden." Pastor Blair sat back in his chair. "Quite a feat, if ever I heard one."

Something in the pastor's voice nudged Haden to pay attention. He lifted his gaze from the Bible and raised an eyebrow. "I don't take any credit," he said. "All the glory belongs to God."

"Amen, of course it does." Pastor Blair suddenly smiled. "And I want you to pray about this. There's a small congregation looking for a pastor in the area."

"They wouldn't want me," Haden said, his voice sounding surprisingly like a yelp. "I'm a convict. I'm in prison."

"A day pass is all you need."

"And I'd sure look pretty going for an interview in my prison suit."

"Just pray about it, Haden. If it's God's will for you to do this then He will iron out the details. Where is your faith?"

"Okay," Haden held up his hand, "I don't want to be accused of not trusting the Lord, but I can't see it happening."

Two weeks later, Haden still couldn't see it happening, even as he stood outside the church doors wearing a practically brand new blue suit and polished black shoes.

[46]

How Pastor Blair managed to find the clothes in his size, Haden didn't know. He adjusted his tie once more, wiped the beginnings of a sweat from his brow, before stepping through the entrance.

I chuckled, remembering the scene. "We were in the middle of an unscheduled prayer meeting when in stepped this mammoth of a guy who'd look more at home in a wrestling cage," I said, "until we looked into his eyes and saw the Spirit of God."

"But he was a convict," Jane sputtered. "How could you trust him?"

"You're forgetting something," I said. "Paul the Apostle spent most of his ministry in prison. He wrote numerous books of the Bible, and had visions."

"But—"

"And Paul was a murderer before his conversion," Faith added. "How many husbands, wives, and innocent children did he cast into prison and to their deaths because of their faith in Christ Jesus?"

"You're right," Jane acknowledged the truth, her incredulity fading away. "So what happened to Hades, I mean Haden?"

"Well," I began, relishing the opportunity to give glory to Jesus, "he shared his testimony with us, leaving out very few details about his parents' deaths, his uncle's abuse, his life in foster care, and then his own criminal activity. But then he moved onto the good stuff, when Jesus turned a sinner into a saint."

I finished off my coffee, remembering the tears that gathered in Haden's eyes that day as he explained how God the Father adopted him, washed him clean of all his sins, and made a new man of him. It was enough to make any grown man bawl like a baby.

I sniffed.

"We didn't vote for him on the spot," Faith said, "but there was a lot of eye catching as each of us there caught the vision that the Lord gave us. By the time Haden finished talking, the Lord had confirmed in all our hearts that here stood a man who'd travelled an ugly, harsh road but he was to be our pastor. No doubt about it."

"Amen," I contributed my approval to her statement.

"Because he was only out on a day pass, he didn't have much time to do anything more than give us his testimony and references."

"By the end of the week, after much prayer, we let the prison know we wanted to hire Haden."

"Change was coming," Faith said as she refilled coffee cups. "We were open to anything the Lord had for us; we wanted Him to do a new work. And not that numbers count, but our congregation went from two hundred to two thousand in the matter of months."

"That's incredible." Jane shook her head in disbelief. "If God can take someone like Haden and put him in the pulpit, what else is God able to do?"

I smiled into my coffee mug as I raised it to my mouth.

"What?" Jane asked, her eyebrows rising. "You have another story for me?"

"All kinds," I said with calm assurance. "You have time?"

"All kinds," she repeated earnestly.

The Prodigal Son

Prologue

"Anyone hear from Harry?" Pastor Haden asked the group of men sitting around the table. We'd met in the church's conference room for our monthly board meeting and thirty minutes into the hour we still hadn't been able to discuss church finances and other matters on account of one of the member's absence.

A chorus of "Nope" and "Uh uh" went around the table.

"What about you, Mike?" The pastor looked expectantly in my direction. Considering Harry and I'd been close friends since high school, if anyone had known where he was it should be me. However, I couldn't solve the mystery either.

"I've called his home but his wife doesn't know where he is." I shook my head. "And he's not answering his cell phone."

"Well, that leaves us with one of two options," the pastor said. "We can go ahead with the meeting without Harry, or we can postpone it until someone hears from him and find out when he's able to make it."

"Give me until tomorrow," I said. "I'll find out what's going on."

When I returned home that night, Faith's face was pinched with concern.

"Harry Emerson's wife just called," she said before I had a chance to tell her why the meeting ended earlier than usual. "It seems Harry has jumped off the edge of the world and disappeared. Do you know anything about this?"

"Nothing." I frowned for what seemed like the hundredth time that night over the same question. "This is insane. Harry is the most dependable guy I know. I think we'd better pray."

Together, we sat down at the table, held hands and lifted Harry to the Lord. We'd just concluded our prayer with an 'amen', when the phone rang.

It was Harry.

"What's going on?" I asked, keeping my tone neutral. "Everyone's concerned. Including your wife."

"I'm home now. Can you round up the board members and the pastor tomorrow afternoon? I'd like to meet with them for coffee."

"Shouldn't be a problem," I said, dismayed that the solution to the mystery surrounding Harry's strange absence continued to elude me. We hung up a moment later and then I put my wife's mind at ease.

"I can't imagine what's going on with him," Faith said. "This just isn't like him.

"Guess we'll have to wait and find out tomorrow." I reached for the phone again and called the pastor.

Harry Emerson fidgeted with his soiled napkin while waiting for pastor Haden and the board members at the coffee shop. A lot of things happened since yesterday morning, things that left him feeling slightly disoriented, and a whole lot anxious.

His reputation at his church might be jeopardized by what he was about to tell the pastor and board but that was the least of his problems. The more pressing one was that the life of a young man, one he'd never known or met, lay in the balance.

As the minutes ticked by, his restless fingers reached for the salt and pepper shakers.

"Can I get you more coffee, sir?" the waitress asked.

Harry glanced up in time to see the pastor and the other men entering the coffee shop. "Could you bring a pot of your best brew and seven mugs?"

"Sure." The look she gave him questioned his sanity, seeing that he was alone, until the men greeted him and took seats at his table. Then she hurried off to do as he'd asked.

"Is everything alright, Harry?" the pastor asked, sitting beside him.

"Yes and no." Harry grimaced, setting the spice shakers back in place on the table. "I'm going out on a limb and making a confession to you, my brothers in the Lord. What you decide to do with the information is between you, each other, and the Lord."

"Absolutely." Pastor Haden took a mug when the waitress set a tray of coffee and cups down. He filled it, and then passed it to another board member. He repeated the action until all the men had coffee, the pastor being the last.

"Brothers," Harry began after clearing his throat, "I've known most of you for many years. I've worked hard, going to university to get a degree in business. I own two successful businesses, and many properties. It's been my honor and pleasure to host talks with the congregation about Biblically sound financial principles."

"You've blessed us all more than we can ever tell you," Pastor Haden said with a nod of gratitude.

"But it all means nothing, if I—" Harry cleared his throat again, as if struggling for the right words, "—If I don't reach out to one very important young man. Someone who doesn't know I exist yet."

Harry lifted his gaze and could tell he'd piqued the interest of the other men. His grin lacked humor. "Most of you might think I've never done much wrong. That my life is my family and work. Now it is. But that wasn't always the case. I've fallen short of the glory of God many times, and one wrong choice in particular not only affects me, but affects the lives of my family and…others."

Raising his hand to hide the lower half of his face, Harry closed his eyes. He appreciated that the other men didn't try to ask questions, or interrupt his flow of thought. He needed to concentrate on what needed to be said.

If he'd have known years ago that a simple act of disobedience and rebellion could bring about such disaster, he'd have been a much better son.

Chapter One

[Thirty Years Earlier]

"Harry, do you know the answer?" the high school math teacher asked from the front of the room.

Slouched at his desk, Harry turned his eyes to the chalk board where the algebraic puzzle waited for his attention. He'd been daydreaming and staring at the girl sitting one desk over in the next aisle. She had the prettiest blonde hair and bluest eyes...

"Harry?"

"No...no ma'am," he stammered as she tapped the black board with chalk.

"Figure it out," she said, her voice tight with impatience. "And sit up straight."

A few of the students laughed as he changed his position in his seat. Heat filled his face when he noticed the pretty blonde had turned and looked at him. However, the small, shy smile she sent him lacked mockery.

"Uh, uh, yes ma'am." He tried to concentrate on the black board but it was difficult when those blue eyes watched him. For the next two minutes, which seemed like an hour, Harry was able to come up with the answer. Good thing he had brains. Otherwise, Mrs. Pentington, infamous for her sour disposition, would have sent him to detention for a week.

When the bell rang, ending that awkward class, Harry sprinted for the door. By rights he should have been the teacher's pet, given his high I.Q. and acumen for numbers, but his deep-seated rebellious nature kept him just slightly at odds with any one in authority.

"Harry."

His fingers stilled, resting on the combination lock before turning to face the person who'd called his name. The blonde girl from his math class smiled a deeper version of the one she'd given him earlier.

"Yeah?" He affected a nonchalant stance, leaning against his still closed locker.

"Just wanted to tell you, great save back there." Her blonde hair swished over her shoulder as she indicated math class. "Mrs. Pentington was itching to give you detention, but you pulled it out of the fire."

A grin prodded his lips. "Thanks."

"I'm Amelia."

"Harry."

"Yeah, I know." She laughed. "So, um..." She shifted the small pile of books in her arms and offered him yet another smile. "A friend of mine is throwing a party this weekend. I just thought I'd let you know, in case you were interested in going."

"Yeah, sure, thanks," Harry said, stunned by the invitation. Everyone knew Amelia was friends with the cool kids in school. She could have had her pick of any of the guys. Not that he was ugly or anything, but she was pretty enough to win beauty pageants.

So why did she choose him?

"Don't worry about bringing anything," she said, "refreshments provided."

And by refreshments, Harry knew, it meant that beer and drugs would flow like water.

Harry had every intention of accepting Amelia's offer. However, the biggest obstacle would be his father. Going out on Friday night wasn't a big deal, but keeping his whereabouts a secret would be the challenge. He'd have to talk to his buddy Mike and see what he could do for backup.

Friday night didn't arrive fast enough to suit Harry. By early evening he'd showered, shaved, and changed into his Sunday best black cords and white and black shirt.

"Where are you going?" his father asked as Harry descended the stairs. An opened Bible rested in his lap as he looked over the top of his glasses while waiting for an answer.

It was a question Harry had expected and prepared an answer for.

"Out." Harry pretended a casualness he didn't feel. He stopped at the hall mirror and checked his hair. "Mike's having a couple friends over. Is that going to be a problem?"

Sometimes, like now, it was difficult to keep the sneer out of his voice. Why couldn't his father be cool like his friends' parents?

"Not for me, but are you sure you're meeting at Michael's?" His father's raised eyebrow set off an alarm in Harry's head.

"Why?"

"Michael's grandfather passed away this afternoon. He and his family left an hour ago to stay with his grandmother."

Harry cursed under his breath. Now he'd have to come up with something else to get his old man off his back.

"So, I repeat, where are you going?"

Years of unspoken mutiny rose within Harry's heart. He was sick of being told where he could go, who he could hang around with, and how to fold his hands properly to pray. In one moment, the wall that kept his anger and resentment in check came tumbling down.

"To a party, Dad," he said, relishing the freedom in his sharply spoken words. "I'm going out and meeting up with a girl."

"What girl?"

"One who has more fun with a bottle of Jack Daniels than a hymnal." Once started, Harry couldn't stop his tirade. "She wears short skirts and make up. And I like her."

While Harry spoke, his father slowly put his Bible aside and stood up. Harry stood well over six feet tall, but his father was taller. Some people might have been intimidated by the harsh expression on the older man's face, but not Harry. His father never put his hands on him in anger.

"I don't know this girl," his father said in a soft voice, "so I will wait to make up my mind about her, but son, you're making a big mistake. You should find a godly young woman to spend time with."

"I'm not interested in those 'godly' young women," Harry said, sneering at the idea. "They're closed-minded, and don't know how to have fun."

"The kind of fun this other young lady seems inclined to have," Mr. Emerson said carefully, as if weighing his words. "She's on a bad path."

"Thought you were going to wait before passing judgment." Harry pulled on his jacket.

"I am," his father said, "But I'm not stupid either. I know what happens to people who get involved in drinking parties before they're twenty. They become alcoholics."

"I don't care."

"Maybe you should, Harry," his father said, an unspoken warning in his voice. "She is on a very destructive road, and if you're not careful you're going to go with her."

"Maybe I want to," Harry thundered. "Maybe this is what I've been looking for all my life."

"If you cared for her, you'd pray for her soul." His father's words followed him as he stormed out into the dark night.

Maybe his father was right, but all he cared about was seeing where the party would lead. And having fun for a change.

"Can I get you another drink, Harry?" Amelia asked. They stood outside on the porch together, music blasted from inside the house. The air was chilly, a slight breeze promised rain, but

Harry didn't notice anything except the presence of the pretty blonde beside him.

"No, thanks, I'm fine." And for good measure, he finished smoking the cigarette she'd handed him a few minutes earlier. It wasn't his first. He'd bummed smokes from school buddies often enough to acquire a taste and to look cool.

"I like it here," she said, glancing up at the darkened cloudy sky. "It's peaceful."

"When there isn't a party going on," he quipped.

"Right." She laughed and looked down at her feet as if suddenly shy.

"So, why'd you invite me here tonight?" It wasn't a question Harry intended to ask that moment, but the drugs he'd taken earlier had loosened his tongue. "You don't even know me."

"I liked what I saw," she said. "You don't act like a jerk."

"Scored big points there, huh?"

"You have no idea." She looked up and suddenly reached out, letting her hand slide down his arm before taking his hand. Harry didn't know what to expect, until she said, "So, you want to see the upstairs?"

He let her lead him back into the house where people smoked, drank, and laughed at nothing at all. Other teens reclined on the floor in a drunken stupor, some shared marijuana. The rest swayed in time to the psychedelic music playing over the house stereo. They were quickly forgotten when Amelia opened up one bedroom door, and turned and looked at him with unspoken meaning in her blue eyes.

Even though he'd never been around people of this caliber he could say with all honestly that this was his kind of fun.

Sometime late into the night, the music stopped. Harry heard pounding on the door, and when he cracked one eye open he saw flashing lights through the open window.

Great. Some one had called the cops, and Harry knew exactly who that someone was. It'd be just like his dad to track him down and cause trouble.

Amelia stirred beside him on the bed, just as one of her friends burst into the room announcing that the police were looking for Harry.

A half hour later, a still high Harry stumbled into the door of his father's home.

"How did you find me?" Harry slurred the question.

"I called one of your other friends," his father said after the police officer left. "Apparently this party has been in the works for quite some time."

"Well you're too late, Dad," he said, heading for his bedroom, "I had fun tonight. The kind of fun you don't want anyone to have."

"You're my son, Harry." He ignored the anguish in his father's voice as he stomped up the stairs. "I've done the best I can to protect you."

"You don't have to protect me from anything, old man. I can take care of myself."

Chapter Two

Harry groaned against the pain ripping through his head as he pulled on a pair of clean socks. His stomach rebelled against the thought of breakfast, his tongue stuck to the roof of his mouth, and he couldn't remember much of what happened the night before. But it was worth it.

Amelia was worth it.

His first thought was to call her. The second was to meet up with her. The third, get high again and have more fun.

However, tracking Amelia down proved more of a challenge than he'd expected. She'd never given him her phone number. Just his luck her last name was Smith, and there had to be at least two hundred listings for Smith in the phone book.

He decided to drive back to the house where the party was held the night before. He knocked at the door. Despite what had gone on less than twelve hours earlier, it didn't seem right to walk in unannounced.

"Yeah, Amelia's here." The guy who answered looked and smelled in serious need of a bath. And a haircut. And a toothbrush. "She's in her room."

"Thanks," Harry said, moving past the other teenager. He trotted up the stairs, his memories of the layout of the house dodgy but there weren't many doors to choose from on the second level. His first guess was right.

Amelia's blonde hair spiked out on the pillow where she huddled under the covers on the bed. Harry vaguely remembered leaving with her in the same position the night before.

"Hey, sleepy head," he said by way of greeting. He sat down next to her on the bed and gently touched her hair. "Time to get up."

"Go away." Her voice last night had been soft and feminine. The one she used that morning was anything but.

"Come on, baby, I missed you." The corners of his mouth kicked up as he tugged on her hair. He'd never felt so free with anyone in his life. "Get up and we'll go do stuff today."

"I said leave me alone." Her hand came up and slapped at him.

"I thought we'd go to the park," Harry said, getting up and opening one of the bureau drawers, rummaging around for clothes for her. It was an intimacy he felt free to have.

"Look, Harry," she said, managing to prop herself up into a sitting position, bracing her weight on her arms. "You're a nice guy. I had lots of fun last night, but I'm not interested in a relationship with you."

"What?" The bureau drawer slammed shut when his weight fell against it. Harry couldn't have been more shocked than if she'd punched him in the stomach.

[59]

"I'm a free agent." She ran her fingers through her hair, squinting against the glare coming in through the window. "This is the kind of life I lead."

"Well, it's not what I'm interested in."

"What interests you isn't my problem. Now if you'll just leave, I can get back to sleep."

"I'm not going anywhere until you explain this to me."

"Fine." A yawn split the lower half of her face. "If you're going to be a baby about this. Here's the facts."

For the next fifteen minutes, Harry listened to Amelia. She told him about her family life, and the kind of abuse that was foreign to him. Sure, his father could be a killjoy most days, but he wasn't like the man who'd brought Amelia into the world.

She told him about being raped as a thirteen year old by her father. Of getting drunk for the first time at the ripe age of fourteen, and of a jealous mother who didn't care what happened to her daughter when she kicked her out on the street.

If it hadn't been for friends, she most likely would have died.

"I learned to take what I could get," she told him, her eyes swollen from a night of drinking and not enough sleep. "And it just so happened, you were something I wanted. But not now. So just go away, Harry."

"I can't believe it," he said finally when she stopped talking. "You aren't like that." He ravaged his hair with shaking hands.

"Better believe I am," she said, pulling the quilt back up around her neck. "The sooner you do the quicker you can get back to the real world."

"It's just the drugs talking," he said.

"If you think so." She shrugged. "Now be a dear and close the door on your way out."

Harry spent the rest of the day driving around town, his thoughts a clutter of confusion. He couldn't believe that Amelia had used him. How could a girl give herself to a guy if she didn't even like him? It didn't make sense.

With renewed determination, Harry figured he'd give Amelia time to come to her senses and apologize for making the mistake of trying to cut him loose. And he'd forgive her, he decided with a grim smile.

At least having the same classes he'd see her. He'd work on her until she got her head on straight. All that other stuff about her father raping her didn't matter. He loved her and they could put it all behind them, get married after high school and have a family. Life would be perfect.

However, Amelia didn't even look his way during class. The odd times he tried to speak to her in private were as equally unsatisfactory as when he'd talked to her the day after the party.

"Go away, Harry," she finally said, her anger rearing up in her blue eyes. "Stop badgering me. I told you I don't want you showing up at the house anymore, and I don't want your notes. We're not a couple, and we never will be."

Harry's heart broke a little more each time he saw her meet up with another new guy. Chunks of hope fell around him as they walked away holding onto each other. Maybe his dad was right about girls like Amelia.

But as the days went by, he still held out hope they'd get back together. That hope lasted until Monday morning, three weeks after the party. Harry showed up for class on time, but there wasn't any sign of Amelia. Nothing new there. Sometimes she arrived late.

When Mrs. Pentington closed the door on the final bell Harry knew Amelia wouldn't be at school that day. It wasn't until he passed her locker and saw it hanging open and empty that he realized she was gone. He'd feared she might do something like this. But it didn't make the pain go away.

"What's the matter with you, Son?" his father asked during supper that night. "Appetite gone?"

"Yeah." Harry poked his mashed potatoes with his fork before he said, "Dad, why do girls run away when things go wrong?"

"You're asking me that?" Mr. Emerson chuckled. "How do I know anything girls do?"

"It's their first line of defense," Mrs. Emerson said, surprising both men. "What?" she asked at their astonished expressions. "It's true. A lot of women don't have the strength to fight, so they run when they're scared."

"Do they ever come back?" Harry pushed his plate away. "You know, from the place they were running from?"

"Sometimes. But only if they have to." His mother sent him a questioning glance. "Why? Who's run away?"

"Just a girl I knew," Harry said, dropping his gaze to the table. "She was in my math class."

"Oh?" His father tried to sound disinterested but Harry noticed the spark of concern in the older man's eyes.

"We weren't friends," he lied. "Just I heard she ran away. Bad stuff going on at home."

"That's too bad," Mrs. Emerson said with a great deal of sympathy. "I hope you're praying for her, Harry. God can work miracles in all kinds of situations."

"Yeah," he muttered, feeling every kind of hypocritical. "Can I be excused?"

Chapter Three

[Four Days Ago]

"Hey, Dad, can I talk to you?" David, Harry's oldest son, stuck his head around the corner of the door leading into the den. Dark brows pulled low over quizzical brown eyes. Harry recognized the look and knew whatever it was on his son's mind was not only important but unpleasant.

"Sure." Harry waved him into the room.

Dressed in full police uniform, David settled on one of the tan leather armchairs in front of the desk and eyed his father with an abnormal wariness. A chill spread across Harry's scalp and slid down his neck.

Funny how life turns out. Harry thought as he leaned back in his leather executive chair and waited for his son to speak. Life had changed drastically after Amelia ran away. When he finally recovered from the hurt she'd left behind in his heart, he'd graduated from high school, and went on to obtain a degree in business from university. By the age of twenty one, he'd started his first business, and made enough money to fund another one.

However nice as money was, it didn't fill the gap reserved for family. So after making amends with his father, getting his life straightened out with God, Harry met and married his wife Gayle.

After a few years it became obvious they couldn't have children so they opted to adopt. Paul was a year younger than David at twenty eight. A quiet boy with a gentle spirit, he'd gravitated to his adopted grandfather. Under the older man's guidance, he decided to become a pastor. He now had his own church in the middle of the city.

Mark, twenty seven, took on the role of vice president for one of Harry's companies. Despite his talent for making money, he made sure power and wealth didn't corrupt his view of life.

Sally followed at twenty six, studying to be a doctor. God had blessed her with a wellspring of compassion for others. No one was supposed to know, but many times she paid for vital medical procedures out of her own pocket anonymously. As a teen, she'd traveled with a church group and ministered to people in Uganda. After seeing their harsh living conditions, she'd decided to do what she could to help as a medical doctor.

And finally Ruth, sweet unassuming Ruth with her lovable smile and command of music. She planned to teach piano and clarinet in school. Surely, the shepherd boy David's soothing praise and worship music couldn't have been any better when she sat down at a piano, her fingers fluttering with butterfly grace over the keys.

If he had to choose, Harry couldn't pick which of the five children made him more proud. They all were exceptional people in his opinion.

"Dad," David cleared his throat, leaning forward in his chair, pressing his fingertips together and staring down at them. If Harry didn't know better, he'd think his grown up son was nervous talking to him. "Dad, did you know a woman named Amelia Smith? She attended your high school for a short time."

Harry's mouth dropped open. He didn't expect that question. "Yes, I did." It was his turn to clear his throat.

"Oh." According to the swirling confusion in David's brown eyes, that wasn't the answer his son was hoping for. "I see."

"Why do you ask?" Harry wasn't sure he wanted to know the answer. In thirty years, he hadn't thought about Amelia, maybe a handful of times. His family and wife filled up all the holes she'd left in his teenaged heart and then some. He'd hate to hear Amelia died. Even felt guilty that he hadn't been a witness to her all those years ago, but he'd been a punk kid more interested in rebelling than the condition of another person's soul.

"It just so happens a friend of mine—Robbie, you remember him don't you?"

Harry nodded.

"Robbie works in the anti-gang division. Seems he's just discovered an up-and-coming criminal in the mafia. A Harry Emerson."

[64]

"What?" Of anything Harry expected to hear, that certainly wasn't it.

"I know." David's laugh sounded contrived. "Robbie thought it was funny, him and you having the same name, you two couldn't lead any different lives." He dropped his gaze again. "It was funny, until…I saw the guy's picture."

Harry's heart dropped to his feet.

"He's your spitting image, Dad." David glanced up again. "Same long, narrow face, same thin build, only thing different is he's got blue eyes."

Amelia's china blue eyes.

"Do you have something to tell me?" David's question echoed from the past, when Harry's father asked him the same thing in regards to Amelia.

Harry nodded slowly. "But I think I should tell everyone at the same time."

Three days later, the entire family was assembled in the dining room. Harry sat at the head, Gayle on his right hand. The kids hadn't been all together in the same room in what felt like years, and Harry regretted that it took something like this to make it happen.

"I don't know where to start," he said, staring down at his coffee mug while his children and wife listened. Shame filled his heart. He hated to think he was about to shatter their estimation of him.

"From the beginning, Dad," Ruth said in her quiet dignified voice that lacked condemnation. "We're here for you. You can tell us anything."

"Thank you." He managed to smile his thanks at her before he began telling them about Amelia, their one night stand, and the possibility they had a brother involved in the mafia.

"Then we've got to rescue him," Sally said, ever the champion for the downcast. "No brother of ours can live like that."

"Amen," Ruth added her agreement to Sally's statement. "When do we meet him?"

"That's just it," Harry said, relieved that his daughters were willing to overlook his past indiscretion and leap to the defense of someone they didn't know; a virtual stranger. "Young Harry Emerson doesn't know I exist."

"Ooh." Some of the enthusiasm left Sally's voice before she chewed on her lower lip. "I guess we just can't go barging into his life."

"Especially not that of an up-and-coming mafia man," David pointed out the obvious. "Good way to get your head blown off."

"Maybe he doesn't want anything to do with you, Dad." Mark put into words what had been going through Harry's head for days. "If he's in the mafia he's obviously not a guy to trifle with."

"But God can make a way where there seems to be no way," Paul was the first to point out.

"Yes."

"That's exactly right."

The others chimed in with their agreement.

"I'd say we have some knee work to do," Gayle said, reaching over to clasp Harry's hand. The kindness and love in her face reminded him just how grateful he was to have her for his wife. And together, as the united family unit they were, they bowed their heads in one accord and prayed.

"And so, my brothers," Harry said to Pastor Haden and the other members of the board, "here I sit, a man with an illegitimate son that two weeks ago I hadn't even known existed. One living in the garbage can of society."

"We'll help you any way we can, Harry," Pastor Haden assured him. The other board members nodded in agreement.

"Thank you." Harry closed his eyes, thanking God for their show of support. "Thank you."

Chapter Four

From his vantage point—the shadowed table in the furthest corner of the restaurant—Harry watched as Mike and Pastor Haden talked to Harry Emerson Jr. on the other side of the room. The two bulking body guards made it clear that any sudden moves from either Mike or the pastor, someone would get hurt. And it wouldn't be they guy they were protecting.

However, Pastor Haden didn't blink an eye at the unspoken warning. He'd spent time in prison; these goons weren't the most intimidating men he'd ever met. Besides, he had God on his side.

David had arranged for the three men to meet that evening. He'd wanted his co-worker Robbie there to protect his dad, in case something went wrong during the meeting, but Harry insisted that everything would be okay.

Harry's gaze slid past to the young man quietly drinking from his wine glass. Although he'd heard David speak of the photos, Harry needed to see on his own to believe he really did have a flesh and blood son.

There wasn't any mistaking it. Everything about him, from the way he slouched in his seat to the rebellious glint in his eyes, shouted that this was Harry's boy.

Boy?

Harry muffled his snort with the palm of his hand. All these years, he'd never known he'd had a son. Amelia had been wrong to keep that information from him. Since learning about his son, he'd had to battle bitterness.

Everything he'd missed. He silently lamented birthdays, holidays, and the opportunity to mold his child into a man. Obviously, Amelia hadn't done that great a job on her own, not if he was on his way to becoming the next crime boss.

As Harry pulled his gaze away from the table and tried to concentrate on the menu, he prayed for his son and thanked God for the support of his family to be there. Despite the fact he'd sin with Amelia during his teen years, his loved ones hadn't condemned him.

All his children had taken a moment to spend some time with him, one on one, after he'd made the announcement to hug and assure him of their love.

The sudden blast of rage from across the room shook him out of his reverie.

"My father died a long time ago." Harry Jr. stood, his fisted hands shaking as he confronted Pastor Haden and Mike. "Take your lies and your religion and get out of here. And don't come back."

Mike turned a look of anguished apology to Harry, and he acknowledged it with a nod. In God's time, they'd meet, Harry knew.

"I'm sorry, Harry," Mike said later that evening when the three men met for coffee at Harry's home. "He's bigger than you'd have thought, making his way up the mafia ranks. He's not a boss yet, but he's getting close."

"Your son boasted about his connections." Pastor Haden laughed as if he knew something the others didn't. "But he's on the losing track. And by losing I mean he doesn't stand a chance against God when his father is praying for him."

"Yeah, I guess you're right." It was exactly the encouragement Harry needed to hear. "Let's get to it then."

After they'd lifted the young man in prayer, Pastor Haden made one last comment before he left. "I've got one more avenue to try."

"I'm glad." Harry grinned. If anyone had connections, it was Pastor Haden.

For two days, Harry stewed and prayed for the man who'd made a mess of his life. Obviously, he'd inherited the same rebellious nature Harry had when he'd met Amelia.

After two more days of intense prayer, he received the call he'd been waiting for.

The man on the other end of the phone took a long time asking the question. "Is this Harry Emerson?"

"Yes," Harry said, his palms suddenly slick with sweat.

"My mother—" The man cut off his explanation with a vile curse.

"Is this Amelia's son?" Harry asked, taking the lead.

Another long pause.

"Yeah."

"I'd really like to meet you," Harry said.

"I'd…like that too."

"Look, I have a house down by the lake." Harry gripped the phone tighter, afraid that if it got away from him he'd never get another chance like this one to talk to his son. "Do you want to maybe…fish?"

"Sure."

Harry gave him the address and when they hung up after making plans for that weekend, he was filled with elation and rejoicing. God had given him favor with his own son.

The lake house was a two storey home habitable in any season. Harry liked it for its solitude and relaxing atmosphere. He'd worked out a lot of business plans here.

And he hoped it wasn't where his family would find his body. One never knew what went through the mind of a mafia man; one with the possibility of a huge chip on his shoulder and a gut full of rage.

Needing a chance to unwind before the younger Harry arrived, Harry opened his tackle box and straightened up the multicolored fishing baubles. That chore completed, he checked the fishing lines making sure they were strong.

The sound of tires over dirt and gravel alerted him he was no longer alone.

Harry didn't know what kind of reunion to expect. He stood in the doorway of the shed and watched as Harry Jr., alone and equally vulnerable, slammed the car door shut and made his way towards him. They stared at each other, noting the family resemblance.

Neither man spoke, but Harry opened his arms, and the younger man didn't hesitate to step into them. Their reunion garnered a lot of tears and even more discussion.

"I couldn't believe it when your son, the cop, told me about you," Harry Jr. said much later that day as he adjusted the line of his fishing rod where the two men sat in lawn chairs on the wharf. "All my life, Mom told me my father didn't care about us. She finally told me the truth before she'd died last year."

When would the lies stop? Harry wondered but he didn't interrupt the younger man's version of the facts of his life.

"She told me she had too many emotional problems, that she'd left town to get away from my father and never went back to him. I was born nine months later."

The sun was setting, the best fishing hours of the day gone, but neither of them cared. They were having their first father and son bonding time.

"Last year, she finally admitted the truth to me. That my father wasn't dead like she'd always made me believe and that he'd loved her, but didn't know I existed."

"I wish I had known about you, son," Harry said, his heart heavy at the loss.

"Me too." Junior sent him a sidelong look, one filled with the longing of a little boy.

They spent the weekend fishing and talking; their hearts open and brutally honest with each other. With candidacy came inner healing. The shared anger the men had for Amelia's lies dried up and blew away in the wind.

"I dropped out of school when I was sixteen." Junior kept his eyes averted from his newly discovered father. "The mob took me under their wing, gave a punk kid protection." He shook his head slowly. "Thought that was something, considering I'd come from nothing; a kid with a crack addicted mother and the busy city streets for a playground."

Each word dropped like rocks in Harry's heart. What he heard described was nothing remotely like the childhood he'd had. So, his father had been strict, but he'd never had to worry where his parents were, if there'd be enough food on the table, even a roof over his head. The blessings he'd taken for granted had been denied his own child.

"I had a quick mind," Junior went on to say. "I caught one boss' attention and he apprenticed me. Through him, I learned the inner workings of his business."

Harry didn't know what to say to that, so remained silent.

"I had my first casino at twenty." Junior snorted, shaking his head. "I must have inherited your intelligence."

Harry desperately wanted to take the young man into his arms and hug away the wasted years, to give his biological son hope. It hurt to think that when Junior had been a kid, instead of playing baseball with his father and reading comic books, he'd found the means of survival in the sludge pits of humanity.

"A year later, I had two restaurants on the upper east side, and a strip club."

Junior hunched his shoulders as if chilled from the breeze coming off the lake. "I wanted to be more than a snot-nosed kid from the streets. And now I am. There's nothing I have to beg for. Just one snap and it's mine; women, money, drugs. Not that I've acquired a taste for drugs, but some of my clientele enjoys them, and you have to keep your customers happy."

Harry opened his mouth to condemn his son's illegal activities, but something stayed him. Now wasn't the time to put a wedge between them by reproving the life style he'd been thrust into. This was the time to show his son love and establish family ties.

"So, Dad." Junior sneered. "Now you know what a waste of your DNA I am."

God, give me wisdom, Harry sent the prayer heavenward. If he didn't choose his words carefully, he just might lose his only chance to make amends for his teenaged rebellion and build a bridge between him and this man; his son.

"You're not a waste of anything, Junior," Harry said, putting his hand on his son's shoulder. Of anything he might have said, by the look in the younger man's eyes, that wasn't what he'd expected. "In fact, you're a gold mine of family inheritance."

"Oh yeah?" Junior smirked but didn't shake off Harry's hand.

"You have your mother's blue eyes, for starters," Harry said. "They were the first thing I noticed about you."

Junior sniffed and turned his face away but still didn't break physical contact.

"And then you have my lanky frame. Were you any good at basketball?"

"Yeah, right. Grace wasn't built into my genetic code."

"I tried out in high school. The coach suggested I give football a chance." Harry blew out a breath before grinning. "Nearly started a war between the two coaches. So I settled for the debate team instead."

Junior gave a grunt that could have been interpreted as amusement.

"That one gave me the verbal skills I needed to face the business world." As if remembering just how different their lives were, silence fell between them for a few more moments. "Sorry, I digressed."

"No, it was…cool."

"Getting back to you," Harry said. "You've got your grandmother's blond curls and your grandfather's determined chin."

"Are they still alive?"

"My father is. Mom died of heart failure after I finished high school."

"I'm sorry."

"Me too. She would have adored you."

"When can I meet my…" Junior's face contorted with emotion but he regained control over himself before he continued, "My grandfather?"

"Anytime you want." Harry nodded to his son. "He knows about you." He remembered the conversation he'd had with his father about his indiscretion with the girl he'd been discouraged from attending the party with years ago. But his father, being a true man of God, never expressed a word of anger towards his grandson when he heard the full story. "In fact, he's eager to meet his newest grandson."

Chapter Five

That evening, after they'd eaten their fill of grilled fish and potatoes, they sat on the deck in the cool evening air. For a while, neither of them spoke. They'd both learned a lot about each other that day. Harry wished Amelia hadn't kept her pregnancy hidden from him. He could have taken his son and raised him in a good home without the boy witnessing the seedy side of life until he'd been much older.

But that didn't guarantee his son would have done anything different with his life, Harry thought, remembering his own short-lived rebellion that resulted in so much loss.

"So you're a business man, huh?" Junior grunted with mirthless laughter. "Who knew the apple wouldn't fall far from the tree."

"Hmm." Harry didn't point out the major legal differences between their career choices.

"I've got connections, you know," Junior said without arrogance. Facts were facts. He knew people. "Anytime you need something, I can put you in touch with someone."

"Thank you for that generous offer," Harry said, keeping his tone neutral. "But over the years I've learned that the best connection to have is the one with Heaven."

"Oh, you're one of those." Junior turned his face away but his tone lacked disapproval. Harry had a feeling his son had investigated him thoroughly before he'd made contact. He also would have discovered that all his business dealings were above board and he'd been more than successful with every venture he'd gotten involved in.

"Yep, one of those," Harry said, grinning.

"And how does that work?" Junior asked, leaning back in his chair and closing his eyes as if he wasn't interested. Only the clenching of his hands on the arms of his chair gave him away. "Does God give you inside information?"

"I was a rebellious kid, son," Harry began. "My father, a very wise and godly man, knew I was headed for trouble if I didn't straighten up. But what did he know? He was from a different generation; he preferred reading the Bible to going out and carousing. They don't come any more boring than that."

"Yeah," Junior agreed but something in his tone indicated he wasn't as hard hearted as he'd like people to think.

"And then I met your mother." Harry released the air in his lungs slowly. "She was beautiful. I fell in love with her the moment she asked me to go to a party with her.

"When my supposedly clueless father figured out what I was about, he advised me to be careful. He didn't judge your mother, but he knew enough about life and what could happen when young men were reckless."

Junior didn't respond this time.

"I thought Amelia and I were meant to be together, but she had other plans." Harry allowed himself another moment to mourn over what could have been, but then remembered the blessings he had now; Gayle and their children. "She must have run when she discovered she was pregnant. I don't know if you've ever lost someone you loved, but it does something to a young man. It either crushes your heart or you take a step back, examine your life, and straighten up."

"You straightened up obviously," Junior surmised.

"After I figured out my dad wasn't as dumb as I thought." Harry glanced down at his feet. "I decided to give God a try, handed over my life to Him, He put the pieces back together, and then I finished my education."

Another bout of silence fell between them.

"I never forgot about your mother." He felt he needed to say that. "There were times I wondered where she was, how she was, and if she needed any help."

"She had issues," Junior shrugged. "Stuff in her past that messed her up."

"I know. She told me." Harry didn't want to remember how she'd explained the abuse she'd experienced in her own home to him. The punk kid he'd been hadn't known how to help someone who'd endured physical and emotional trauma. But the man he'd grown into did.

"So now I've come along and messed up your wholesome image." The bitterness in Junior's words was tangible.

"Believe me," Harry said, resting his hand on his blood son's shoulder, "You haven't messed up anything. You're a gift God has given me in my old age."

Junior opened his mouth as if to repudiate that, then quickly closed it and looked away. Harry wished he knew what was going through the younger man's mind but didn't pursue it. He'd give the boy time to digest everything they'd discussed.

"This weekend has gone by too fast," Harry said, breaking the silence. "I'm a greedy man. I want more time with you."

Junior didn't respond beyond a sniff and Harry knew his son was crying.

"Can we do this again soon?"

"Yeah." Junior's voice sounded strangled as he swiped his nose with the back of his sleeve. "Yeah, I'd like that."

"Good. Now can I press it and ask you to consider coming to church with me sometime?" As an extra bonus, he added, "You'd get to meet your grandfather."

"We'll see."

"You should have seen the bass he caught," Harry nearly shouted into the phone the next evening from his home office. "It had to have been three feet long."

"Oh, those fish stories," Mike said, teasing. "So you two had a good time."

"Fantastic!" Harry quieted down suddenly. "We talked about God, Mike."

"He let you? That boy of yours was pretty adamant when Pastor Haden and I met up with him at the restaurant."

"Junior needed some time with his dad," Harry said. "He didn't sound disgusted at the idea of going to church with me."

"Then we'll re-post his name on the prayer chain," Mike said with confidence. "Your boy doesn't stand a chance."

By the following Sunday, Harry and Junior had talked via phone every evening, hours of getting acquainted that meant so much to both of them. It cemented their bond, and friendship, and the discoveries they'd made about each other made them laugh and cry.

No more mention was made about Junior attending church that Sunday, but Harry didn't let up praying about it.

That Sunday, Harry stood at the glass doors of the church long after the greeters had left to sit with the rest of the congregation. The thunder of voices raised in a worship song filled the air. He'd wait there all morning if he had to, Harry decided with determination. He'd wait there every Sunday waiting for his son, as the Father had waited for His Prodigal.

"Dad?"

Harry recognized David's voice behind him. He turned and smiled at his son; the one he'd watched grow up, play sports, date, and get married. Harry wished he'd had just such an opportunity with Harry Junior.

"He's probably not going to show up," David said, touching his father's shoulder in a way that spoke volumes of their own parent and child relationship. "Why don't you come in and sit with the family?"

"I will, in a while," Harry said with a gentle smile. "You go on back."

But David didn't leave. It became obvious he didn't intend moving from his father's side. They didn't talk, just waited.

When a couple of the church's young girls got up to sing a special, Harry watched as a car pulled into the filled parking lot.

And not just any car, it was the top of the line Cadillac, black with tinted windows. And Harry Junior was driving.

Joy leapt within Harry's heart. He didn't wait until his son finished parking the car, he ran out to greet him. After they shared a hug, Harry had the pleasure of introducing his first born to his other son.

"David's the one who found out about you," Harry said, watching with pride as the other men shook hands.

"I guess I owe you," Junior told David.

"That's what family does," David said, grinning.

Obviously they looked nothing alike, not having the same DNA link. Both men tall, but David dark and stocky where Junior was thin, and blond, but they had Harry in common and it was the first step towards forming family bonds.

The men entered the church together and sat in the pew where the other family members waited them. The siblings were curious, the girls sent Junior welcoming smiles and the boys nodded in silent greeting. Harry squirmed in his seat like a kid counting down the days to a holiday. He couldn't wait for them to be properly introduced.

When the singing special ended, Pastor Haden took his place in the pulpit. A month ago, it'd been requested he give his testimony and he chose this morning to do just that. Harry realized then just how much the pastor's and Junior's lives paralleled each other.

Grinning, he shook his head and marveled again at God's perfect timing.

As Pastor Haden testified to the abuse he'd endured as a child, his involvement with gangs and finally how God let him see Hell in a vision. It was that vision that had awakened him to the truth of the Gospel, to the reality of Heaven and Hell and the eternity of them both.

Praying that the words impacted his son, Harry cast a glance in Junior's direction.

What he saw melted his heart and brought a fresh rush of gratitude within his soul. Harry Junior had his head down but it was obvious he was weeping. Tears rolled down the young man's cheeks and fell on his neatly ironed tan colored pants.

Harry knew the Holy Spirit was convicting Junior's heart.

Then the pastor gave the altar call. Many went forward, including Junior.

As one, Harry, Gayle, and their five children surrounded Junior at the altar, laid hands on him and prayed while he surrendered his life to the Lord.

Mike grinned through his tears. "That was quite a day."

"Amen," Faith agreed wholeheartedly. "I don't think there was a dry eye in church that morning."

"Didn't any of his other children feel threatened?" Jane asked, blowing her nose into a facial tissue.

"Nope." Mike shook his head, wiping his eyes on the back of his sleeve. "If you saw them together, you'd never know they hadn't grown up together. The unity in that home is incredible."

"A true miracle," Faith said.

"What happened to the life Harry Junior had with the mafia?"

"Gave it up," Mike said, reaching for his coffee cup. "Just like that. God brought him out without any one so much as turning a hair. That's a miracle too. Normally, the mafia doesn't let anyone go."

"Well…" Jane gripped the tissues in her hand and glanced over at Mike, "We can't stop now. I need to hear more testimonies of people in your church!"

Jo-Jo's Trip

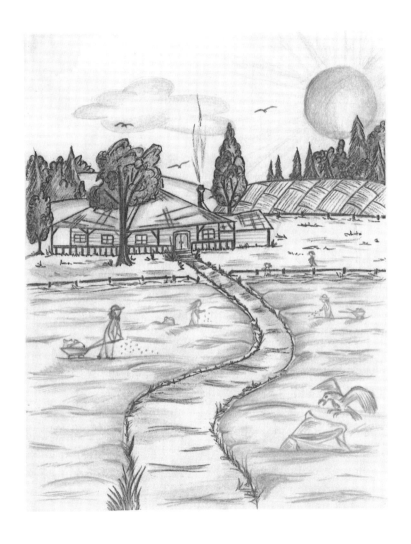

Chapter One

Joanne woke that morning feeling the full potential of the day hit her full force. The sun streamed in through the open window in her bedroom, not quite making it to her bed. She stretched before tossing aside the pink and white comforter.

After she showered, dressed, and read her Bible and prayed during breakfast, she sorted through the day's priorities. First off, she'd have to call her favorite people in the world—after her father, of course—Mike and Faith, her second parents. They'd want to hear the news directly from her mouth.

She'd known them since she was very young. They'd lived in the same neighborhood before they had their children. Mike and Faith were as loving to her as if she'd been one of their own. It made growing up a little easier after her mother died and her father struggled to raise a little girl alone.

Because of Mike and Faith, she'd attended their church and gave her life to Christ Jesus. And because of their encouragement, she'd moved to Prince Edward Island to attend university to study nursing.

"Hi Aunt Faith," Jo-Jo said, wrapping the phone cord around her index finger. "How's everyone?" Masking the excitement bubbling up within her proved to be a challenge.

"Just great, kiddo." Faith's familiar voice came over the line. "What about you?"

"Well," Jo-Jo dragged out the word, "I got something to tell you."

"Okay, honey," Faith said, as if bracing for the worse. "You can tell us anything. We're here for you."

"Hey, it's not bad news." Jo-Jo laughed. "In fact, it's spectacular."

"All right then."

"I'm moving to Vancouver Island," Jo-Jo blurted out then held her breath, waiting for Faith's reaction.

Silence fell between them.

"Hello?"

"I thought you said it was good news?" Faith said.

"It is," Jo-Jo hurried to assure her. "All my nurse friends have headed out there and I know God is calling me to go too."

"Are you sure?"

"Aunt Faith." Jo-Jo laughed again. It was just like her second mother to be so protective of her. "I've been praying for God's will. And for the longest time I didn't hear anything. And then last Sunday during service, out of the blue, He tells me He's got something special for me in British Columbia."

"Alright, Jo-Jo," Faith finally spoke, "I guess if we have to let you go…"

"It's the right thing," Jo-Jo said. "I can feel it. I can feel it!"

They prayed together before they hung up. Jo-Jo's hand clutched the receiver a moment longer, a smile lifting her lips. Everything she'd told Aunt Faith was true. God was calling her to Vancouver Island, but first she planned to get more spiritually grounded in the Bible and prayer, and spend time with her family and friends before she went on her great adventure.

Also, she wouldn't be going alone. The pastor had planned a six month motorcycle tour across Canada with a group of people from their church. They'd be street witnessing and serving in soup kitchens during the trek. Though she didn't own a motorcycle yet, she'd signed up for the tour months ago. But in God's time, as was His way, He'd supply her needs.

She still wasn't sure what she'd do once she arrived in British Columbia—aside from putting her nursing education to work—but without a doubt she knew God had plans. All she needed to do was remain faithful to Him and not get distracted.

The day scheduled for departure, Mike and Faith showed up at Jo-Jo's church for the send off. Jo-Jo had bought a motorbike, granted it wasn't a Harley, she preferred comfort to being cool. A small trailer was included in the deal, and it was packed and secured to the back of the bike.

Seven bikers in total were going, including the pastor and his wife. The stand-in pastor, a young man who'd graduated from Bible school three years earlier, would take his place in the pulpit until the pastor returned.

"I'm going to miss you," Faith said, clinging to Jo-Jo and crying. "The Lord watch between me and thee while we are absent one from another."

"I'll miss you guys too," Jo-Jo said, stepping back reluctantly when her friend released her. "But don't worry, I'll come back to visit."

"You better."

The sound of motorbike engines revving to life made Jo-Jo grab up her helmet from the bike's saddle. She gave her Uncle Mike one last one-armed hug, strapped her helmet on under her chin, and then turned her bike West.

"Good bye." Jo-Jo waved to the well-wishers surrounding the small group of bikers. And then she was flying down the highway. Nothing felt as free or as liberating as riding a motorbike over open highway.

For three hours they drove, but to Jo-Jo time didn't seem to move. When they stopped for the night, the group decided on a motel in the area. They'd already driven for five hours and the mutual consensus went up that they didn't want to tire too quickly, wanting to spend time street witnessing that evening. Too much of a good thing could spoil the enthusiasm, she thought with a grin as she shut down the engine and removed her helmet.

Jo-Jo and the only other single woman on the tour shared a room. The group met for supper at the motel restaurant where they discussed their plans for the following day.

"I have a copy of tomorrow's itinerary," the pastor said, handing out sheets of paper while waiting for dinner to arrive. "I'd like everyone to meet at seven thirty am in the motel's meeting room for prayer and Bible study."

The expected good-natured groans at the scheduled early hour made its round at their table when the waiter brought their food. As one they bowed their heads and prayed for God's continued blessing over their journey and the food.

"Now I've seen everything," the waiter said, the expression on his face comical in its incredulity. "Praying bikers."

"We're having a service at the church in town," the pastor said, then proceeded to give the waiter the address.

"I know the place." The waiter nodded.

"You should come hear us." The pastor winked at the group. "Some of us can sing. Not me, but some of us, like Jo-Jo here."

Jo-Jo felt her face heat up. "I'm not that good," she managed to stammer out.

"Don't listen to her," the pastor said, leaning conspiratorial like to the waiter. "She's a crowd pleaser."

"Hey, you never know," the waiter said, glancing her way. "I just might. Starts at seven, huh?" And he walked back to the kitchen.

"Make sure we all leave the kid a very generous tip," the pastor whispered to the group. "Otherwise everything we just said won't mean a thing."

The party dug deep into their pockets and left a fifty dollar tip in bills and change. It might have seemed extravagant to some people, but when a soul was on the line money couldn't be an object.

The next evening, a fair sized crowd filled the parking lot of the church where the group was holding service. Jo-Jo's nerves acted up a little, knowing she was expected to sing. Why did she always get so nervous? She wondered. It wasn't like she was performing brain surgery.

Nope, it was much more important. She had to surrender her will completely to the Lord's moving, let Him use her voice and song to speak to the hearts of the people in attendance. She knew she had a lovely country western style voice, one with strength and confidence. However it wasn't about her, it was about the One Who gave her the gift in the first place and that He use her for His glory.

The pastor introduced her to those gathered in the sanctuary and she stepped up to the mic. She took a quick breath before she gave a brief description of her trust in God.

"The song I chose tonight is very special to me," she began, letting her gaze scan the audience. She smiled when she recognized the waiter from the restaurant. "It's more a reminder of Who I follow and why. The words have spoken to my heart during the darkest times of my life, and lifted my eyes back to the Lord Who promised never to leave me nor forsake me. And He never has."

The pre-recorded music played and Jo-Jo closed her eyes as she sang.

That night ten people gave their lives to the Lord, and two other couples asked to join their travels. Their love for lost souls quickly earned them a place on the tour.

Chapter Two

Jo-Jo lay in bed and stared up at the ceiling of the motel room. Over the course of six months, the rented rooms had pretty much the same look. But the lives touched by the services they'd held in various churches were as different as the snowflakes that had fallen on the prairies while they'd passed through.

Every time an altar called had been given, new names were added to the Lamb's Book of Life. Each story varied by degrees of heart breaking detail, wounded lives, broken dreams, abuse, drugs. The list was never ending. But the rebirth of hope and joy in their eyes remained the same. And always, after the pastor gave the reason for why the group was there that evening, more people wanted to join the tour.

By the time the group arrived in Vancouver City, the number of the people in their motorcycle tour had grown enough to make a Christmas parade seem minute.

The city wouldn't know what hit; she laughed to herself before falling into a deep sleep. The following morning, they met for prayer at the next church where they'd minister that evening. The motel meeting rooms could no longer accommodate the tour's host of bikers.

"Well, I have to say," the pastor said as the women of the church served them breakfast. "These months have gone by faster than I would have believed possible. Tonight, will be our final service together as a group."

Jo-Jo felt the beginnings of tears burn her eyes. Could it really be the end of their togetherness? They'd experienced a lot of life on the Trans-Canada, seen lives changed through the power of Jesus Christ, served meals to countless homeless people, and shared the gospel with those who desperately needed hope.

It was an experience Jo-Jo wouldn't trade for a million dollars. She let her gaze linger on each face she'd come to know and love. They were her family. Some were taking flights back home to the Maritimes by the end of the week. Some she might never see again this side of eternity. But they all had a place in her heart.

Apparently, by the show of emotion working the muscles of his face, the pastor felt the same way.

"God has blessed us during this tour. We've gotten to meet and know everyone traveling with us. You all mean so much to

Linda and I." On cue, his wife reached over and held his hand. "This is an experience we'll never forget."

"This is just a foretaste of Heaven," Linda said, taking the time to let her smile reach everyone seated at the tables. "And I can't wait."

Amens echoed around the large room.

"That being said, I want to remind everyone we'll be breaking up into four groups and ministering in soup kitchens around the city."

Jo-Jo smiled down at the plate of scrambled eggs and sausages placed before her on the table. Of all the things she enjoyed most, it was serving meals to the homeless, rummaging through donated clothes for them, and sharing with them the Gospel of Jesus Christ.

After breakfast, Jo-Jo grabbed up her purse and met with the others in her group. It'd be the last time she'd have this opportunity, but the day was open to new possibilities. She'd called one of her friends before leaving the motel that morning, a nurse from her university who'd moved out to Vancouver Island months ago. They planned to meet at the soup kitchen and get caught up on things. However, Marjorie was on the sidewalk when Jo-Jo arrived with her group.

"Hey, Jo-Jo." Marjorie gave her a tight hug. "I can't tell you how surprised I was when you called. But I'm glad you did."

"Me too."

The mission opened its doors then and Marjorie announced she was there to work with the group. "Can't get rid of me that quick," Marjorie teased, donning an apron with the rest of the group.

Her friend's willingness to lend a hand didn't surprise Jo-Jo. Marjorie had given her life to Christ before she'd migrated to the Island.

They didn't have much of a chance to talk freely until break time. They both carried their trays of homemade soup and rolls to one of the few empty places at a table near the back of the large room.

"What ever possessed you to join a motorcycle group and tour Canada?" Marjorie asked. "I just can't picture you in a helmet."

"It was in God's plans for my life," Jo-Jo said with a big grin. "When the pastor announced the idea of the tour something in my heart told me that was exactly what I needed to do. And, well, here I am."

She went on to explain experiences she had at various churches, the lives touched by the power of the Holy Spirit and how the motorcycle group continued to grow.

"I've never met such precious people before," Jo-Jo said before biting into the buttered roll. "And it's opened my eyes to a lot of the suffering in my own country, made me determined to help as many as I can when possible."

"I feel the same way about nursing," Marjorie said, nodding with understanding. "To see sick people get better, children smile again." She shook her head. "Wow, it's amazing. But then you know all about that. Girl, when are you going to settle down and work with me?"

"I'd like to see the hospital before I apply for an interview," Jo-Jo said. "Is that possible?"

"I'm off today, but I could get Tanya to meet you, give you a tour."

"That'd be incredible."

"She was sorry she couldn't be here this morning, she had to fill in for one of the nurses on vacation. Tanya is a little out of her depth on this floor," Marjorie said, rolling her gaze to the ceiling. "Or so she says, but you know her, she doesn't like change."

"True," Jo-Jo agreed, laughing. "I'll drop in after we've finished at the soup kitchen and see her."

"She'd love that."

Marjorie was right. Tanya was waiting at the elevator when Jo-Jo arrived at the hospital. She'd used Marjorie's cell phone to make arrangements to meet with her. Tanya squealed with excitement when she saw her friend. They hugged and laughed.

"Are you really going to get a job here?" Tanya asked as if she couldn't believe her ears.

"If I get hired."

Tanya squealed again. "You're going to move in with me. I share a two bedroom flat with another girl, but the place is big enough for all of us."

They reminisced as Tanya gave Jo-Jo the tour of the hospital. It was a relatively new building with an airy concept. Huge windows looked out into the well-cared for gardens, the hallways were spacious, and the brilliant light from the windows and environmentally friendly light bulbs combined to give one the feel of perpetual summer.

Jo-Jo knew it'd be the perfect setting to work in.

"And we have a solarium upstairs," Tanya said. "I usually take my dinner there during break hour. It's very peaceful." She grabbed Jo-Jo's arm and squeezed. "I can't believe you're here."

"You should have been with us during the motorcycle tour across Canada," Jo-Jo said. "You would have had the best time."

"That really does sound like an adventure," Tanya said with regret. "You're right, I wish I could have been with you during that road trip. However, I've been having my own adventures right here."

Something in Tanya's voice alerted Jo-Jo that something was going on. Something important.

"What do you mean?" Jo-Jo asked.

"This is the floor I've been working lately, covering for a nurse on vacation," Tanya said, not quite answering Jo-Jo's question. She greeted another nurse in scrubs by name and then continued down the hall. "I've never worked with people in comas before."

"Comas?"

"Yeah." Tanya nodded. "I'm used to caring for babies on maternity ward, and I guess in a way this is kind of like a maternity ward. These people are completely helpless, unable to do anything for themselves. They can't communicate what they want, but you know in a way it's a little creepy too, especially when you know they just might be able to sense you in the room and hear what you're saying."

"I see your point."

"But in a way it's more rewarding than working with babies," Tanya said. "I know, I don't like change but in a way this change has been good for me." She paused at one door. "Like this guy, for example. John Doe."

Jo-Jo looked into the darkened room, the curtains were drawn. It was empty except for the thin figure lying on the bed hooked up to a ventilator, feeding tube, and monitor.

"He'd jumped off a bridge a few weeks ago," Tanya whispered the information as they entered the room. "No one expected him to live. Fact is he had no I.D. on him when rescue workers brought him here, so we can't contact his family to let them know about him."

Jo-Jo moved closer to the bed while Tanya pushed the curtains open. She gazed down at the man's pale, thin face and gasped.

"I know him," she said.

"You do?"

"Well, he's lost a lot of weight, and his hair is whiter but I'm sure it's him."

"Who would have thought," Tanya shook her head, "That you, of all people, could identify someone a million miles from home?"

"That's the funny part," Jo-Jo said, shaking her head. "He's from Prince Edward Island."

"No way!"

"What would bring him here?" Jo-Jo wondered out loud. "Why come all this way just to jump off a bridge?"

"That's another mystery," Tanya said, looking over the machines to make sure everything was running properly. "Think you can solve it?"

"I can't, but I know someone who can." Jo-Jo smiled with confidence.

Chapter Three

"More bikers joined the tour last night," Jo-Jo said into the phone in the motel room that evening. "That brings it up to four hundred now. I'll be sad to see everyone leave, but I'm exactly where God wants me to be."

"I can see that now," Faith said, sounding every bit as amazed as Jo-Jo. "I didn't at first, but after listening to you. God's ways are amazing."

"Aren't they though?" Jo-Jo twisted the cord around her index finger. "And the pastor tallied up the number of people who gave their lives to the Lord. Between our stops at soup kitchens, church services, and street witnessing, over five thousand people made decisions."

"There must have been a constant party in Heaven." Faith laughed. "I can picture it now."

"I knew you'd be just as excited over this," Jo-Jo said with confidence. "I also have another reason for calling."

"Oh boy, the last time you said that you announced you were moving to the other side of the country." There was a definite note of dread in Faith's voice. "Don't tell me you're moving to China now."

"Hah, no!" Jo-Jo giggled. "It's more a prayer request. I've landed a job interview tomorrow at the Vancouver Island Hospital. Please pray I get a position. And something else…"

"What is it?"

"I'm not free to discuss details right now, suffice to say there's a man in a coma at the hospital. And get this, he's from P.E.I. but that's all I can say right now. If you could get the prayer chain started, I'd really appreciate it."

"Done."

Before they hung up, Faith prayed for blessings over the younger woman's job interview and the man in the coma and then Jo-Jo went to bed. It was with a heavy heart she fell asleep that night. For the past six months she'd been a part of the motorcycle group, and forged the deepest Christian ties to these people. To think that the end of the tour was over and she wouldn't see them again for a long time, if ever, made her sad.

Of course, tomorrow would open another chapter to her life, but still…

Before going for her job interview, Jo-Jo stopped by the church to give her farewells to the tour.

"This is it, Jo-Jo," Linda, the pastor's wife, said. Her smile was a mixture of sadness and joy. "We're leaving and you're going to find out about that job at the hospital."

Why did life mean you were always saying goodbye to someone you loved? Jo-Jo wondered as she shared prayers and hugs with her original group from Prince Edward Island. She watched in silence as they put their helmets on, revved their engines, and drove away. Until they were out of sight, she waved goodbye.

Then Jo-Jo turned toward the city just as her bus rounded the corner and made its way to her stop. She didn't know the city enough to take a chance on driving her motorbike to the hospital.

The interview went well. In a month's time she'd start her new position. In the meantime, she planned to return to Prince Edward Island to collect her things. She also planned on doing a little bit of investigation during that time.

When the plane landed in Moncton the following week, Faith and Mike met Jo-Jo at the airport. They hugged and talked about her adventures all the way back to their home.

"You wouldn't believe the experiences I've had," Jo-Jo said. "Just when you think you can't meet any more beautiful Christians, God just leads another one to you."

"That's the way He works," Faith said, her eyes twinkling.

They sat down to eat supper together. Faith had prepared lasagna and garlic bread, and cherry cheesecake for supper. Jo-Jo closed her eyes and savored every bite.

"You're the best pasta cook alive, Aunt Faith," she said.

"It's edible," Mike teased. Faith slapped his arm playfully but laughed.

"By the way," Jo-Jo said, breaking a piece of garlic bread into bite size pieces. "Do you remember that guy, the one who'd been a pilot during the Gulf War?"

"Do you mean Ken Bishop?"

"Yeah, that's the guy." Jo-Jo hit the heel of her hand to her forehead. "I couldn't think of his name."

"Funny you should ask," Mike said, a thoughtful expression on his face. "We haven't heard anything about him for months now. It's like he fell off the edge of the planet."

"Why do you want to know?" Faith asked.

"He's the guy in Vancouver, the one in the coma."

"Why would he be there?" Faith asked.

"He was born there," Mike supplied the answer. "He only moved to P.E.I. after he got out of the forces. Married. Had some kids."

"How do you know him?" Jo-Jo asked.

"His mother-in-law went to our church for a while," Mike said as if carefully weighing his words. "She requested prayer for Ken. He attended a service once three years ago at Christmas."

Jo-Jo knew Mike was hiding information from her. It didn't seem right to be discussing Ken and yet she truly wanted to help the man lying helpless in a coma back in a hospital in British Columbia.

She stayed with Mike and Faith that night and the next day caught a bus to the Island. Her plans spun through her mind as she made her way back home. Once she finished packing, she planned to meet with Ken's children, to let them know what was going on with their father.

"I don't care if he rots in a hospital bed," the first daughter said with venom, shocking Jo-Jo. "My only regret is he survived the jump. And if he has the misfortune of pulling out of it, you can tell him that for me."

Jo-Jo didn't so much as have an opportunity to comment before the door was slammed in her face. Wow, what a hard hearted person, she thought.

Ken had four children, and three of them reacted exactly the same way; making it clear how much they despised their father, and hoped he died because he was already dead to them.

However, the youngest daughter ushered Jo-Jo into her small home. She was a pretty girl with short brown hair and hazel eyes. Jo-Jo hoped she wouldn't get the same reception. It grieved her heart that a man so alone in the world could be shunned by his own flesh and blood.

With true Island hospitality, Ken Bishop's daughter made coffee and invited Jo-Jo to sit down in the kitchen even after learning Jo-Jo had news of her father.

Once they each held mugs of coffee, the daughter began talking. "It's not that we never loved our father," Shannon said, staring down at the table. "It's just that he never gave us the time of day. He spent all his money on booze. Mom had to work two jobs just to keep a roof over our heads and food on the table. It was nothing for Dad to take money from her purse; when it came down to the good of the family and his alcohol, well, his liquid mistress always won."

Jo-Jo listened, her heart growing ever heavier with the story that the daughter told. Her own relationship with her father hadn't been an easy one, not since losing her mother, but they loved each other and would sacrifice anything for the welfare of the other.

"We tried, we really did, to get close to Dad." Shannon's gaze stayed fastened on the crumbs she'd swept into a small pile on top of the table. "But he didn't want it. Something happened to him even before he went to the Gulf during the early nineties."

Shannon sighed, as if the weight of the world was on her shoulders. "When he came back he made a name for himself in the community, and not a nice one. He had such rage, and if any one tangled with him they often came out of it learning a few lessons and gaining some stitches and maybe even a cast. Dad had little mercy for anyone weaker."

"I'm so sorry, Shannon," Jo-Jo said, reaching out to touch the other woman's hand. "But surely you want to see your Dad. He's not in the position to help himself."

"No, I don't," Shannon shook her head. "I've been hurt enough by that man. He didn't deserve my mom. She was too good for him. My family and I have all made our peace with the rejection we felt from him. We've grown up and moved on. We're not going to let him back in to destroy our lives again."

Jo-Jo could understand Shannon on one level. However, she couldn't stop picturing Ken lying in the hospital bed, every bit helpless as a newborn baby. Alone. Unloved.

"I've bothered your family enough," Jo-Jo said, finishing off her coffee and reaching for her purse. "I'll leave my number, just in case you change your mind."

"I won't. None of us will," Shannon declined to accept the card Jo-Jo held out to her.

Jo-Jo dropped the card onto the table. "You never know. If you do, I'll answer any questions you might have about your dad."

Shannon nodded but kept her eyes averted.

Chapter Four

Packing done, surplus furniture sold off, Jo-Jo returned to Vancouver Island. She wished she had better news to tell Marjorie and Tanya. They were happy to now have a name to put on their patient, but saddened at his family's response to his being in a coma. Their faces reflected the same sorrow Jo-Jo felt. Ken Bishop was truly alone.

"He has us," Tanya said as if the Holy Spirit put that determination within her soul. "We'll be his family."

"Good idea," Marjorie agreed. "We can spend our break time with him, talking to him, praying over him."

The three agreed to be his adopted family.

For the next two weeks they met during break as planned. They read Scriptures to Ken, Tanya held his hand, and Marjorie prayed softly. Jo-Jo found an old CD player, brought it in and played praise and worship music soft enough that only Ken could hear it.

"Keep praying for Ken, Aunt Faith," Jo-Jo urged. "The doctors aren't holding out much hope he'll pull through."

"Of course. What's that, Mike?" Faith put her hand over the phone and her husband's voice in the background was muffled. She came back to the phone and said, "Wait a second, Jo-Jo, Mike wants to talk to you."

"Hey, kid," Mike greeted her. "I wanted to tell you something that the Lord has revealed to me a few days ago. It's concerning your friend Ken."

"Okay." It was funny to hear Ken referred to as her friend, considering she had yet to have a conversation with the man. But she was open to anything her Uncle Mike had to tell her.

"I was reading the Bible," Mike began. "When God showed me that Ken is like a fig tree. He'd been rejected by everyone, his family, he didn't have any friends, and his life was barren. He doesn't have the capacity to love anyone, himself included. God then told me he wanted His people to be like farmers, to cultivate the soil around the fig tree, to trim the branches, and to have mercy on something that anyone else might have thought was ugly. God sees a beauty in Ken's life that we can't see with our minds. But if we're faithful to show mercy to him, God will reveal His plans for Ken's life."

"Wow, that's amazing," Jo-Jo said, completely blown away by what the Lord had shown him. "I can't wait to tell Tanya and Marjorie. They're going to be stoked. Maybe even more so than I am."

During lunch break during her shift the next day, Jo-Jo related what Mike had told her over the phone.

"I think we've been doing that," Marjorie pointed out. "By spending time with the ol' guy," She rubbed his hand and smiled. "Don't you think so, Ken?"

The girls jumped when Ken's leg twitched.

"Did you see that?" Tanya whispered as if afraid to speak too loud for fear of jeopardizing whatever was happening to Ken.

"I did." Marjorie stood and stared down at his legs as if she'd seen a mirage.

"Me too." Jo-Jo drew out her agreement, afraid to breathe.

"I'm getting the doctor," Marjorie said before rushing from the room.

"You won't believe what happened today, Aunt Faith," Jo-Jo said into the phone Friday night.

"What?"

"He woke up," Jo-Jo shouted the news. "Ken woke up."

"Jo-Jo, praise the Lord, that's incredible."

"It is! It really is…"

A sudden pause filled the air.

"But…" Faith prodded.

"He has amnesia. Doesn't remember a thing, his name, nothing."

"Maybe that's for the best."

"Why do you say that?"

"Perhaps he needs to forget the life he once lived, and start fresh."

"Maybe." Jo-Jo sighed. "The doctors also discovered he's got bone cancer. He needs a bone marrow transplant if he's going to live."

"Oh, dear."

"So could you activate the prayer line again?" Jo-Jo asked. "My prayer group is lifting him up to the Lord too."

Jo-Jo's prayer group consisted of Tanya, Marjorie, other nurses, doctors, and generally anyone who worked at the hospital who was a Christians. They met every Wednesday in homes of the people who attended their meetings. The purpose of the meetings was not only to study the Bible and pray together but also to keep each other accountable. They encouraged one another concerning different situations that arose at the hospital, particularly patients whom they felt needed prayer.

Ken had been on their prayer list for a long time and when he'd come out of the coma there was a great deal of rejoicing among the Christian staff followed by concern for the bone cancer.

"We'll need to pray for a donor," Marjorie said. "I'd sure hate to see him die now that he's awake."

Jo-Jo knew the feeling. "If God is using Ken for His glory wouldn't He heal him?"

"And what about his family?" One of the doctors pointed out later in the hospital dining room. "They don't sound like the kind of people that'd welcome him back with open arms."

"You can't blame them for that," Tanya said. "He was a menace in the community and to the ones he should have loved best in the world."

"Well, God's got plans," Marjorie stated, unfazed by their negative input. "And I say we have another round of intercessory prayers to see Ken not only shake off the amnesia, but that his family makes a place in their lives for him."

"Amen," the others seconded.

For the next month, an unbroken prayer chain formed across Canada, linking up in agreement for a man his own family turned away from in his greatest hour of need. Jo-Jo felt inclined to fast for the man. On her weekend off from work, she spent the entire time in the presence of the Lord seeking His face and His will concerning Ken.

When she returned to work on Monday it was to face a bouncing Marjorie with a smile that spread across her face.

"He asked me to read the Bible to him, Jo-Jo," she said. "I figured once he regained consciousness he wouldn't want to hear it anymore, but he did. That's a good sign isn't it?"

"Really?" Jo-Jo's tears spoke of her happiness. The emotional rollercoaster Ken had put her on was wild, but she wouldn't have missed it for anything. She peaked into his room without announcing herself.

"He's resting right now," Marjorie said, whispering. "But he'd asked me if he'd imagined hearing someone pray and reading the Bible while he was in the coma."

"Then he was aware." Jo-Jo nodded before turning away. "Praise God, we were able to minister to him when he couldn't lodge a complaint against us."

Marjorie laughed. "If you'd have seen him telling it this morning, you'd think we were angels sent from Heaven to comfort him."

"His heart is tender before the Lord." When she prepared to leave for her floor, Marjorie held her arm.

"He said he loved the prayer and Bible readings, but what touched his heart most was the singing."

"Well." Jo-Jo couldn't speak around the emotion constricting her throat. She blinked hard, nodded, and would have made a complete fool of herself in front of the other nurses at the desk if Marjorie hadn't pulled her through the open door.

"Oh, come on. I want you to meet him now." She released Jo-Jo's arm when she strode to open the curtains. "Time for him to take his medication now anyway."

A pale Ken was sitting up on his hospital bed, the color in his face was better than it had been while he was immobilized but it remained waxy looking. His eyes came to life when Marjorie introduced Jo-Jo to him.

"Hi, Ken," Marjorie greeted him with a greater depth of warmth in her voice. "I brought you a surprise. This is my friend Jo-Jo."

"So you're the girl who sang," he said, his grey eyes suspiciously damp. He held out his hand to her and she took it. "You have a beautiful voice, but it was the words of those songs that made me realize there is a God. In fact, you three girls—" Tanya entered the room at that moment, "—have shown me a kindness that I have a feeling I don't deserve. But it was appreciated."

"We've been praying for you," Marjorie said. "A lot of people have been."

His smile was weak but genuine. "Thank you, girls." He paused, as if fighting for composure. "I know you've already done a lot for me...but, I have one more question. Do you know if I have any family?"

The three women shared a knowing look. How could they tell him his own children wanted nothing to do with him? That he'd been such a scoundrel, an entire town feared him?

Instead, with a great deal of diplomacy, Jo-Jo said, "We're working on it." And they were, with prayer.

They stayed a few more moments, making sure Ken was comfortable, before they went back to their stations.

For the next six months, Ken endured grueling sessions of physio. The accident and coma had left him unable to walk unaided. Jo-Jo, Tanya, and Marjorie had forged a friendship with him, and he was always excited, like a child, to share that day's progress with them. And, as always, at the end of the meeting, he asked if they'd found his family yet.

It was getting harder to hide the truth. Guilt tore through Jo-Jo's heart every time, but she couldn't be brutally honest with a frail old man.

As the weeks passed, and his strength returned, the work load increased. Jo-Jo, Tanya, and Marjorie soon didn't have as much time to dedicate to their favorite patient. However, their ministry didn't go unrewarded.

"He gave his life to the Lord, Aunt Faith," Jo-Jo said, sounding suspiciously bouncy like Marjorie when she made the announcement on the telephone. "Ken got saved!"

There was a definite sound of tears of joy when Faith relayed the information to Mike. He usually hovered near Faith whenever Jo-Jo called, waiting for news about Ken.

"And that's not all," Jo-Jo continued above their celebration, "He's going home."

"What?"

"He's regained his memory, and has been in touch with one of his daughters. They're going to meet. He really wants to make amends to his family for what he put them through."

"Then I guess the prayer chain isn't finished with him yet," Faith said.

"Nuh uh," Jo-Jo said, smiling. "The hospital in P.E.I. have matched him up with a donor, he'll be flown back home and have everything looked after there."

"God is so good," Faith said, sounding awed.

"He is that," Jo-Jo agreed, taking a deep breath. "And more."

Epilogue

"I got a letter," Jo-Jo announced, waving an opened envelop as she and her best friends ate their lunch in the solarium.

"Who's it from?" Marjorie asked before biting into her chicken sandwich.

"Ken."

"Read it, read it!" Both Tanya and Marjorie urged.

My dearest girls at the hospital;

You'll never know how life has turned out since I woke up in that hospital room. I praise God you never gave up hope for a stranger, one who isn't worthy to have survived that jump from the bridge.

But God has done a miracle in my life, and for that I am eternally grateful to Him.

I don't know how it happened, but my wife and I are back together, my children and I are working towards healing as a family. They were there while I went through the surgery and now the treatments. I never knew I could cry so many tears. And they are all of gratitude and thanksgiving.

God bless all of you.

Your brother in Christ Jesus,
Ken.

P.S. I've apologized to people in my town, ones I've hurt, and a few have given their lives to the Lord on account of what He's done for me.

The girls remained silent for a long moment, lost in their thoughts.

"Did you ever think it possible," Tanya said, shaking her head slowly, "That God could take a man like Ken and restore him to his family and community?"

"Who knew what God's plans were when I started out on a road trip not even a year ago." Jo-Jo smiled. "That I'd get to see such an incredible miracle."

"And I have a feeling you're just seeing the beginning," Faith told her over the phone that night.

"I know we should go," Jane said, reaching for a fresh tissue, "But I want to hear more. What's Jo-Jo doing now?"

"She continues to minister to people she comes in contact with at the hospital," Faith said, crossing the room to the sink, "Be it a cup of cold water to a bedridden patient or leading someone to Christ in the chapel."

"She sounds like a precious person."

"Yes, she is," Faith agreed, sounding choked up. She sniffed, and wiped her suspiciously damp eyes on the back of her sleeve. "Now, no arguments, you're staying for supper."

"We can't impose," Jane protested.

"Nonsense. We're just having meatloaf and mashed potatoes."

"Well, if you're sure."

"Absolutely." Faith made the decision final with the nod of her head.

"Do you need help with anything?"

"Not a bit."

"Then tell me another story," Jane begged.

The Fighter

Prologue

"Are you sure I'm not intruding?" the man on the passenger side of the half ton truck asked, his face creased with equal parts concern and sun damage. "I mean, it's your parents' thirty fifth wedding anniversary, man."

Paul Emerson turned a grin on the other man as he parked in the already filled driveway. His sisters and brothers had arrived before him, but what was five minutes between siblings?

It didn't matter that of the six children, five were adopted. Their parents, Harry Senior and Gayle Emerson, never treated any of them differently. Granted Paul's father hadn't found out about his blood son until a short time ago, but even then, no one's feelings towards each other had changed. They were family, end of story.

"Well, you can go on home if you want, Tommy" Paul said. "But you'll be missing out on the best turkey dinner with all the trimmings. And I won't even mention the blueberry pie. Mom's known for her culinary expertise, but hey—"

"You had me at all the trimmings," the other man said, his hand on the door release. "Let's go."

Another victory, Paul chuckled quietly as he led the way to the front entrance of his parent's two-storey brick house. Despite his father's business sense, the family had been brought up to live a little bit above miserly. That meant they had money to share with those in serious financial need, in their community and church.

The house was bustling with activity. Paul's sisters, Sally and Ruth, were helping their mother in the kitchen. He could hear them chattering about nonessential girl stuff like clothes. Some things never changed, he noted with a grin.

It was the men's voices that drew Paul and Tommy into the den. His brother, David, and newly found brother, Harry Junior, sat in the arm chairs opposite the oak desk where Harry Senior leaned back in his office chair balancing a ball point pen between his fingers. A habit he had whenever he considered a business venture.

"Hey, it's the reverend," David teased, standing up to give his younger brother a hug.

"That's Mister Reverend to you, Officer," Paul joked back. "Glad to see we haven't missed dinner."

"Who's your friend?" Harry Senior asked before Paul had a chance to make introductions.

"This is Tommy Gardner," Paul said. "He was speaking at my church this morning, gave his testimony."

"Hey, I know you," David said.

Tommy glanced at the off-duty officer and stepped back in time; forty years to be exact.

Chapter One

"Say uncle," Jake said. He pushed the squirming, smaller boy's face into the dirt and pressed his knee into his back. "Come on, say it!"

"No!" Twelve year old Tommy resisted, despising his own weakness but hating his oldest brother even more for his cruelty.

"You wanna stay like this all day?"

"I don't care," Tommy said, continuing to struggle.

"Jake, get off your brother." A mean, slightly slurred voice shouted from the open doorway of their house. "I need you to run to the store and get some beer."

"This ain't over, squirt," Jake hissed before he released his brother and sauntered over to their father.

Tommy shook his arms trying to get the blood flow going again. If he'd given in, the abuse would only have escalated. Even at his young age he knew that. It hadn't always been like this. Before his mama moved out, she'd made sure the older boys left him alone, he was her baby. But when she ran away with a neighbor, Tommy was suddenly defenseless against his stronger, bigger brothers.

Tommy glanced over where their father handed Jake some money and knew if he didn't get out of there soon one of his other siblings would take the opportunity to beat on him. After a quick look around, Tommy struck out for the woods in behind the house. Once there, he'd be safe. Too bad he couldn't bunk out there all the time, he thought with regret.

One day soon, he vowed, picking up a stick, he'd run away to his mom and no one would ever pound on him again.

Once deep enough in the woods, and confident he hadn't been followed, Tommy dropped the stick in a heap of other sticks he'd fashioned into arrows with his small pocket knife during his free time. He spent most of his days here, and some nights. He'd even built an almost unnoticeable fort out of branches and broken tree limbs. It offered enough space for him to lie down if he decided to sleep there. He'd stolen a small camp stove from a hardware store, a feat he still prided himself on, the sleeping bag he'd taken from someone's clothesline, and the food he smuggled from home.

If his brothers weren't such creeps, Tommy might have shared his camp with them. But as it was, he enjoyed his solitude. There was a lot less pain that way.

Tommy settled on hotdogs and marshmallows for his supper. Nothing tasted better when eating in the outdoors in peace. He didn't find peace at home. There, he'd have to watch his father get lost in a bottle and ramble on about his glory days in the army. Without adult supervision, Jake would lock Tommy in another strangle hold until he finally caved and begged for mercy.

Nope, Tommy decided as he took a big bite of his hotdog, he was better off alone at his fort.

Around eight o'clock that evening, he heard Gerald, his second oldest brother, calling for him to come home. Tommy grinned from the comfort of the sleeping bag in his fort while reading comic books and drinking soda. No way was he going to interrupt this happy moment by answering the call.

Normally, when one of the boys yelled for him to get home they stopped after about twenty minutes. Tonight they persisted. Tommy turned the flash light on his wrist watch. The yelling had been going on for about two hours. And now three other male voices had joined Gerald's.

This was odd. Tommy's stomach did a little jump. Something wasn't right; otherwise they'd ignore his absence.

Without stopping to reconsider, Tommy cleaned up his fort, grabbed his flashlight, and ran carefully through the trees. He knew the path perfectly, knew each hidden stump and rock, and knew when to duck his head.

When he reached the edge of the trees, he paused. Sure enough, his two brothers and a few of their neighbors were shouting his name together. Staying in the shadows, he made his way around the house.

"What's goin' on?" he asked with all the innocence he could muster.

"Tommy!" One woman, a neighbor, wrapped her arms around him. "We were scared to death when you didn't answer."

Tommy forced himself not to struggle within her embrace. He didn't want to hurt her feelings but he also hated it when anyone held on to him like that; anyone not his mother. Besides, his arms were still sore from the hold Jake had on him earlier that afternoon.

"Where were you, squirt?" Jake demanded, poking him in the ribs.

That was the kind of reception Tommy was used to, and he didn't like it.

"Never mind that, Jake," Gerald said, taking the lead. "Hey kid, got some bad news. Dad's dead."

"What?" Tommy yelled. Of anything he expected to hear, it certainly wasn't the passing of their father.

"You poor boys." The woman who'd hugged Tommy burst into tears. "You never stood a chance from the beginning."

The look on Jake's dirty smeared face said he wanted to tell her to shut up, but somehow managed to restrain himself.

"What happened?" Tommy demanded, feeling the earth shift under his feet.

"The ambulance guy said he had a heart attack," Tommy's second brother, Gerald, explained. Though younger than Jake by three years, he acted more like the head of the family. "The foster people are coming out to get us now."

"I'm not going to no foster home," Jake said, swearing. "I'm leaving now."

"You do that, Jake, and I'm calling the cops right now," the neighbor lady said.

"I'm going to get my stuff," the boy muttered. However, Jake didn't have time to retrieve any of his personal belongings. The woman from foster care services arrived, introduced herself as Mrs. Cook, and hustled them into her car. The boys waited while the woman took a moment to talk to the neighbor.

Tommy watched them without being able to hear what was said, but he knew. He could tell by the expression on her face she was telling them everything about his family, about their drunken father, about the way the boys fought constantly among themselves and with the other children in the neighborhood.

And about their mother running away from them.

A dark cloud of sadness fell over Tommy. He lowered his head and kicked the back of the seat with his torn and stained sneakers, willing away the tears. If he cried now, the other boys would pounce on him and give him a thrashing.

"Gonna cry, sookie baby?"

Too late. Jake had seen the dampness in his eyes.

"Cry, Tommy, cry!" Jake put his arm around Tommy's throat and squeezed until he was gasping for breath.

"Let go!" Gerald's voice sounded even louder in the car's interior. He lunged from the front seat, pulling Jake's arm off Tommy.

The older boys wrangled, fists made contact with jaws, and feet slammed into shins. Tommy squeezed into the corner of the car as far away as possible from the fight. He hated the brutality in his life. He'd give anything just then to be back at his camp, away from the nightmare he'd been plunged into.

"You stop this right now," Mrs. Cook shouted, pulling Gerald and Jake away from each other with a great deal of effort. However, they continued to strike out at each other with their feet. Bruce, the second youngest, grabbed Tommy's hair and made him cry out.

"You're savages," the woman said as if horrified by the discovery. "There's no way you can stay in one home together. You'd tear a place apart in no time."

It was the best news Tommy heard in a long time. Not that he wanted his dad dead, but if it meant getting away from his brutish brothers…

"What about our mom?" Gerald said. "If you call her, she'll get us."

"Who is she?" Mrs. Cook asked.

Gerald gave her their mother's name and phone number. Tommy was shocked they'd had that information. If he'd have known, he'd have tried calling her, begging her to take him with her.

"I'll get in touch with her tomorrow," Mrs. Cook said after jotting down the information on a piece of paper she found in her purse. "Now put on your seatbelts. I've got to find places for all of you tonight."

Tommy was the first to be placed. The people who welcomed him into their home seemed kind, but they could have been putting on a show for Mrs. Cook. Tommy watched as the car pulled away with his brothers before his foster care guardians led him into the tidy, comfortable home. He liked that the carpets were clean, the sofa and armchairs matched, but mostly he liked the television in the living room. It didn't have half an inch of dust on it, and one of his favorite sitcoms was playing.

Despite having hotdogs earlier, he ate the heaping plate of food they set before him on the table; pork chops, mashed potatoes, and corn on the cob. Then his foster mom ran a bath in the pristine tub for him. After that, she gave him a set of flannel pajamas, a size or two too large, with helicopters and soldiers on them. The bed he slept in was warm, comfortable, and clean.

He could get used to this kind of life, he decided with a half smile as he put his arms under his head and stared up at the ceiling. He wondered if his brother had it as nice. And if they didn't, who cared?

He sobered immediately as he remembered his reason for being there. Why'd his dad go and kill himself? Why didn't he see that his drinking made things bad for everyone? Maybe if he'd stopped, Tommy's mother wouldn't have left.

And maybe now that his dad was gone, his mother would get him and take him home with her. That's all Tommy really wanted; to be with his mom who loved him better than anyone else in the world.

Comforted by that thought, he fell asleep.

Chapter Two

Things didn't work out like Tommy expected. For some reason, Mrs. Cook told him she hadn't managed to locate his mother yet, and that he'd have to stay with the Andersons longer than expected.

Adjustments didn't come easily to Tommy. His first day at his new school, he gave another boy a black eye. The second day, he'd put his jack knife to the same boy's throat and was suspended for two weeks.

"Tell me, Tommy, why are you so angry?" the foster care's counselor asked.

"I ain't angry," Tommy said, staring down at the floor. Even at his age, his legs didn't reach the floor when he sat down.

"Well, you shouldn't be," the smiling man said, crossing one leg over the other. "The Andersons are nice people, aren't they? They've given you clean clothes, food, a warm bed. All the things your father couldn't provide you with."

"Did you ever call my mother?" Tommy changed the subject. "I want to see her."

"Yes, I've been in contact with her." He lowered his gaze to the notebook on his lap. "Unfortunately she doesn't have the means to care for you and your brothers."

Tommy scowled. "I'm the youngest." In his mind, that explained everything.

"Your mother," the counselor cleared his throat before continuing, "is having another child."

Another child?

Tommy's head came up at that. Fresh rage swept over him. He was lying! His mother loved him. What would she want with another kid?

"I want to see her." Tommy's determination doubled.

"I'm sorry son, you can't." The counselor seemed equally determined to deny Tommy his one request. "She's not feeling strong enough to see any of you."

Now Tommy knew the man was lying. His mother had always treated him special, cuddling him when one of his brothers hurt him, making sure he had enough to eat. It was on account of his father and brothers she'd left, because she'd never have left him.

"I'll find her myself!" Anger churned in his stomach as he jumped down from his chair and headed for the door.

"Tommy?" The counselor stood up. "She doesn't want you."

For two weeks, Tommy didn't want to believe that his mother could abandon him. But then he got the phone call from her.

"Did you say you didn't want me around you, Ma?" he pleaded, pressing the receiver to his ear hard enough to make his ear ring.

"I'm sorry, baby—"

He didn't hear the rest of her apology. His mind blank, he dropped the phone and ran to his room where he hid under the bed and fought tears with every ounce of his strength.

By the time his foster mother found him, he'd determined in his heart that no one would ever hurt him that way again.

The first day back to school, after his suspension ended, Tommy put the same boy he'd been bullying in the hospital with a broken leg and cracked ribs. The foster system, deeming him a far more difficult child than they'd first thought, sent him to a half-way house for troubled boys.

Tommy continued to make decisions with his fists. His temper put the other boys in the half-way house on the defensive. It soon became clear he was more than trouble, he was a threat to anyone who got in his way.

Five months into the system, Tommy had a growing spurt, suddenly towering five inches over the tallest boy in the house. However, he still hadn't learned to control his anger, and foster care decided they'd try to channel his fury by sending him to a military style boot camp for troubled teen boys.

Tommy welcomed the change. The instructors made it clear from day one that he wasn't going to be bullying anyone. Sporting a new buzz cut, Tommy felt the knot of anger relax. The officers, with their rigid code of conduct and no-nonsense tone of voice immediately demanded his respect. In fact, they intimidated him, but a part of him also knew they'd teach him important things like survival.

He scrubbed his dirty fingernails over the bristles on his head, liking the sensation, before he was ordered to pick up his uniform at the supply office and head for block D.

Tommy shared his barracks with eleven other young men. He had his own locker and cot. It was expected of him to tidy up his quarters, to polish his military issued boots, and keep his uniform spotless.

It didn't take long for Tommy to know the men in charge demanded precision, discipline, a good attitude and instant obedience from each of the boys. And they meant business. Tommy only had to step out of line once to learn he never wanted to disobey his commanding officers again.

A week spent peeling one hundred pounds of potatoes a day, standing up to his arm pits in hot soapy water washing greasy pots and pans, and mopping the kitchen floor wasn't his idea of fun. So obedience came quick.

Tommy lied in his cot one night, arms under his head while his peers slept, and grinned at the ceiling. This was the kind of life he liked. No one picked on him. And when he obeyed commands he was treated with respect.

He was learning life skills that gave him strength, discipline, and focus. The food was decent. The exercise added muscles to his body. At this rate, he'd be the kind of human machine his brothers wouldn't want to mess with ever again, he thought with a grim smile.

"Hey, Gardner," one of the guys who shared Tommy's barracks, shouted at him from across the gym. "C.E.O. wants a word with you."

"Thanks." Tommy lowered himself from the pull-up bar, grabbed his towel and wiped his brow as he headed for the door. When the C.E.O. requested a meeting, it meant now.

"Come in Gardner," The commanding officer beckoned him into the office even as he spoke into the telephone. "Yes, sir, I'll have that ready for you within the week," he said, ending the conversation.

"You wanted to see me, sir?" Tommy asked, standing respectfully as he'd been taught.

"At ease," C.E.O. Shellings ordered. Tommy immediately relaxed his stance, putting his hands behind his back and sliding his feet apart about twelve inches.

"You've been here how long now, Gardner?" Shellings asked.

"Five years, sir." Tommy didn't need to think about the question. He'd finally found what he classified as home. It was here he attended school, graduated with honors, and was working towards becoming a captain.

"That makes you what, eighteen?"

"Yes, sir."

"Good." Shellings nodded as if it was the best information he'd had all day. "You've done very well here, son. I like to think we played a big role turning you into a fit human being and an even fitter soldier."

"Yes, sir."

"So," Shellings drawled out the word as he propped his feet up on his desk, "how'd you like a chance to go Navy?"

That startled Tommy out of his controlled stance. "Excuse me, sir?"

"Yes, you've heard me right." Shillings laughed as if he'd just told Tommy a joke. "The navy is looking for potential Seals and I recommended you. That is, unless you don't think you could handle it."

"I...I'd be honored, sir." Tommy swallowed. It was the greatest compliment he could ever receive. Navy Seal wasn't just a job, it was a lifestyle. And only the cream of the crop stood a chance to reach that position in the forces."

"That's what I thought," Shellings picked up a packet of stapled papers. "I've already done the paper work, you'll leave by the end of the week."

"Yes, sir."

"Dismissed."

Tommy stood outside on the base grounds and looked around, unable to believe the remarkable turn his life took within moments. In a way, he'd be sad to leave the base. It'd been a good home to him, and he was moving up the ranks. But becoming a Navy Seal would be a dream come true.

"Heard the news, Gardner," one of the guys from his barracks said when Tommy entered their barracks. "Congratulations."

"Thanks." Tommy inclined his head in acknowledgement. "Bet you're glad to be out of this dump," another of his bunk mates said. He was a new guy and had the attitude of a street fighter. He reminded Tommy of his brother Jake.

"This is actually one of the best places I've ever been in," Tommy said.

"You're kidding me." The boy looked disgusted. "These guys tell you when to wake up, when to eat, when to shower, and when to go to the bathroom. When the opportunity arises for me to get out of here, you better believe I'm gone."

"Your loss," Tommy said, shrugging. "This is the kind of place where you learn to become a real person."

"You gotta be kidding me," the other teen muttered, "the only thing going on around here is a lot of brainwashing."

Tommy smiled but didn't say anything else.

Chapter Three

[Fifteen Years Later]

"Welcome to Hell Week, boys," Lt. Thomas Gardner greeted the large group of young men as he entered the classroom. They were potential Navy Seals. Each eager expression reminded him of when he'd been their age, starting training. "Only ten percent of you will make the grueling grade. The rest of you are either going to leave limping or wimping. Any of you can drop out at anytime. In fact, I expect you to."

A murmur of protest went through the crowd but Lt. Gardner ignored it.

"Sir?" One of the young men waved his hand.

"I haven't opened the floor for questions," Lt. Gardner stated. "But seeing as your ignorance doesn't know any better, I'll give you this one for free." He peered over the black rim of his glasses. "Take advantage of it. There won't be another one."

"Sir," the young man's voice broke as if suddenly realizing to whom he spoke, "Is…is it true you were with the group of Seals who took out the Somali pirates a few years back?"

"What's your name, boy?" Lt. Gardner asked.

"Koates. William Koates."

"Let me tell you something, Mr. Koates," he said, "It won't matter whose done what if you find yourself on a boat facing the wrong side of a missile launcher. Have I answered your question?"

"Yes, sir." Koates' face flamed amidst the sound of laughter from his peers.

"Now, let's carry on, shall we?" Lt. Gardner said. This was his second year instructing potential Seals. He'd asked for this position after he'd seen combat on numerous occasions and been wounded on his last one. He hadn't been kidding about the missile launchers. His last mission had been exactly that: facing a crew of Somali pirates who'd kidnapped a handful of tourists from their ship with an arsenal of weapons at their disposal. They'd shot the Seals helicopter out of the air, the one he'd been about to jump from, taking a chunk out of his leg.

After countless surgeries and physical therapy, his career as an active Naval Seal was over. Tommy wouldn't consider himself bitter, but he didn't like to be reminded of the incident that had ended the most satisfying time of his life.

"How many of you enlisted for the Seals because of a video game you've played and thought it'd be pretty cool to play dress up with guns?" he asked in a pseudo-friendly voice.

A few hands went up.

"Good." He grinned. Anyone who knew him knew that wasn't a good sign. His voice immediately hardened as his smile fell away. "A lot of young men like yourselves have met a brutal end because they thought the same way. Unlike your game systems, there is no re-set button when you're on active duty. This is it. You fail while you're out on the field and chances are you're not only going to end your odds for survival but those in your company as well and maybe a half dozen innocent bystanders."

He sent a probing glance around the room, noticing the uncomfortable expressions growing on each face. "I see it's starting to sink in," he said, nodding with approval. "Good."

Lt. Gardner hated wasted life. He'd seen enough young men die needlessly and he'd do everything he could to make the ten percent of those in the room the best fighting machines possible.

"I haven't introduced myself properly," he said, sitting behind his desk. "I'm Lt. Gardner; Special Warfare Operator 1st

Class Petty Officer. I am both SEAL and Free Fall Parachutist qualified. I will be your instructor for as long as you are part of this program."

"Cool." A few male voices floated back to him, they were clearly impressed with his rank. Impressing them wasn't important to Tommy. He was there to teach them how to stay alive if they insisted on being Navy Seals.

"Sir?" One of the young men followed Tommy outside into the hall after class had ended.

"Yes?" Tommy glanced down at his watch, quickly growing impatient.

"I...I wanted to introduce myself." The young man averted his gaze to the floor. Tommy suspected he wouldn't make it as a SEAL, but it wasn't his job to weed them out.

"Introduce yourself, Son," Tommy said, aware he was going to be late for a meeting if he didn't get his act in gear.

"Actually, here's the funny part." The boy had the audacity to grin. It vanished the moment Tommy fixed his unblinking stare on him. "I...I'm your brother. Leonard Collicut."

"I have three brothers," Tommy said, his shoulders going rigid. "And you don't look anything like them." That much was true. He and his brothers had dark hair and grey eyes, this young man had red hair and blue eyes.

"Our mom," Collicut explained losing his earlier cockiness. "She and my dad got married and she had my older brother and me."

Tommy narrowed his eyes. "So you think my being an instructor here will give you a leg up over the others?"

He was being harsh and unfair, but Tommy didn't care. He'd faced down death and overcame obstacles that made others respect him. However, the pain from his childhood, and his mother's rejection, still lurked beneath the cold surface. Hearing the kid put into words what he didn't want to acknowledge—that his mother went off and had another family, forgetting that he'd ever existed—infuriated him as nothing else could.

"N...no sir!" Leonard shook his head vehemently. "I wanted to meet you. That's all. You're a hero."

"Is that so?" Tommy softened his voice as he looked closer at the youthful face turned towards him. He could see his mother in the young man's face, see her warm blue eyes, her gentle unaffected smile, and upturned nose. They did nothing to pacify his rage. "Perhaps you'd be so kind to ask your mother," he emphasized your, "Why she thought it natural to leave her sons in an abusive home while she traipsed off with another man?"

"Well, I...I would." Leonard rubbed the back of his head. "But...but she died last year."

The statement snapped Tommy's head back faster than if Leonard had landed a punch.

"How?" Tommy asked through suddenly numb lips.

"Cancer."

Tommy didn't reply. He turned sharply on his heels and strode down the hall. The red in front of his eyes blinded him. He didn't remember getting to his car; only that he gripped the steering wheel fighting the temptation to ram his Bentley into the nearest brick wall.

He didn't know how long he sat in the car, gripping the steering wheel. When the red haze cleared from his eyes, he drove home mechanically. Tommy lived on the outskirts of the city, on a newer cul-de-sac. He chose the split-level, brick house for its homey feel; something he'd never had in his childhood.

After parking the car, and getting the mail—both ingrained habits—Tommy headed for the liquor cabinet in the den with the intention of getting sloshed. And while he did, he called his brother, Gerald, to pass on the 'good news' about their mother.

"Long time no talk, man," his brother's voice came over the line. The last sober portion of Tommy's brain couldn't remember when they'd spoken to each other. "What's going on?"

"Mom's dead."

Silence fell over the line.

"How'd you find out?" Gerald asked finally.

"Met up with our kid brother, Leonard." Tommy laughed, a sound without humor as he brought his shot glass to his mouth. "Looked just like her too."

"Wow, Mom," Gerald said, as if he couldn't get a grip on the information.

"Just thought you should know."

"When?" Gerald asked. "When did it happen?"

"I don't know. She's just dead."

"You sound awful," Gerald said. "Why don't I call Jake and we get together?"

"You know," Tommy slurred into the phone, "That doesn't sound like a bad idea."

Tommy met up with Gerald and Jake at the local casino. The booze flowed as freely as the chips on the roulette wheel. After losing most of his life's savings in a matter of hours—something Tommy would never have done if he'd been stone cold sober—he and his brothers went bar hopping.

"My brother," Jake said, looping his flabby arm over Tommy's neck and knuckling his hair. "The loser."

"I'm definitely a happy drunk," Tommy quipped, chuckling as he raised the glass unsteadily to his mouth. "Who needs anything but this stuff to make you happy?"

For the next six hours, Tommy and his brothers hit the liquor without stopping. The smell that radiated off their drunken bodies kept the waitresses at bay, and that suited Tommy. The last thing he wanted was to be bothered by strangers.

Tommy slammed his glass down on the bar. "We were made for this life, boys," he said. "Beer was in our blood before we were born. It all trickled down the trunk of the family tree. Like sap. Like us. Sap."

"I think we better get someone home," Gerald said, giddy now. "Li'le brother is getting sappy." He broke out into almost hysterical laughter at his bad pun.

Together, the three brothers staggered back to Tommy's expensive car. Tommy fell before he could open the driver side door. Jake stepped over his prone body and got in behind the wheel.

"Come on, kid." Gerald pulled and pushed Tommy into the front passenger seat before he moved around the car and got into the back. "This makes me think of that time Dad was loaded. Ended up, I had to drive the car home."

"That's the night he fell off the porch." Jake joined in with the reminiscing. "Remember, he broke his foot and couldn't buy his booze? He got a cab to bring it out to the place. When the guy wouldn't give me the liquor because I was too young, Dad busted out a window and held the gun on him. I got the beer then." Jake shook his head, guffawing. "Served the guy right when Dad refused to pay for it."

"Those were the good ol' days." Gerald stretched his arms out across the back of his seat and closed his eyes.

"Yeah." The optimism in Jake's voice dropped a degree. "Things would have been a lot different for us, if Mom hadn't traipsed off with that other guy."

"If she'd have stayed, Dad wouldn't have died, and we could have been together." Gerald released a deep breath. "We wouldn't have ended up in different places."

"Who'd have thought Tommy would have ended up in boot camp?" Jake leaned his head back against the head rest and smiled. "He was a gutless wonder. A real pansy."

"Military school," Tommy clarified. "And it made a man of me."

"Ah yes, our hero." Jake's sarcasm pierced Tommy's drunken brain. "We're not worthy to be in the presence of such greatness, Gerald."

"Yeah, well, I got shifted between ten foster homes," Gerald said with a great deal of resentment. "Every one of them had other foster kids, usually ones from the bottom of the system. If I wanted to eat I had to keep my mouth shut."

"Boo hoo." Jake taunted him. "I ended up with a couple who hated the look of each other. They were going to adopt me."

"Did they?" Tommy asked.

"Nope. I made sure of it. They weren't capable of looking after a dog, let alone a kid. Their trailer smelled like a brewery set on a toxic pit."

"It's getting late. We should get back to our motel and grab some sleep." Jake tried to find the ignition with the key. After his third fumbling try he succeeded. It was

nearly three in the morning and the roads were deserted, which was a good thing for them. Had there been traffic, they wouldn't have made it alive out of the parking lot.

Tommy slowly woke up in a haze. It was around midnight, he discovered, squinting at the clock radio next to his motel bed. He clenched his jaw against the pain pounding between his temples.

He pushed himself up from the bed and glanced around. Sure enough, his two brothers were still sleeping. Tommy wiped a hand across his brow, closing his eyes against the agony whipping through his head.

What in the world made him think getting together with his brothers would be a smart thing to do? He wondered. In fact, this was the first time they really ever got along without fighting.

And then Tommy remembered why they seemed chummy. He'd emptied out his bank account, and his retirement fund, to support their debauchery of the past few hours.

And for what? Tommy gritted his teeth as his memory returned. He'd sunk to this level because his own mother had rejected him years ago. Then he shrugged. Who cared if she chose to walk away and start a second family? He'd grown up without her, and hadn't done such a bad job of it. Granted, his choices lately left much to be desired, but he still had his career.

What he needed was to find a good woman and get married. Fill up his brick house with kids. Yep, that's exactly what he needed to do, Tommy decided as he stumbled from the motel room into the parking lot.

He searched his pockets for his car keys and came up empty. Then he remembered Jake left them in the ignition. He needed to get away from his brothers. Gerald and Jake had only been bad influences in his life, and after tonight he'd never talk to them again.

How Jake managed to park somewhat evenly in the parking lot evaded Tommy, but that was the least of his worries just then. Hours of binge drinking were taking its toll on his stomach.

He barely made it to the edge of the parking lot before he expelled what felt like a lifetime of bad booze. Tommy wiped his mouth with the back of his hand and stared, glazed eyed, around him, getting his bearings. He didn't recognize this part of town.

However, before he had the opportunity to find out where he was, the all too familiar sound of a fight brought him staggering around to the side of the motel.

"Stop it. I'll give you the money, man. Just don't hurt me anymore," one man begged.

Holding onto the building for support, Tommy watched as two large men pounded on a much smaller male. It brought back memories of Jake beating him up years earlier. Every bit of rage Tommy felt as a child resurfaced in that moment, spurred him on. He stalked the two men without them realizing it until he was almost on their necks.

His training with the Seals made him dangerous. Getting into a physical confrontation with the general public was illegal. But in his hung-over state, rationalizing anything was limited.

The first attacker got away, barely. The second attacker wasn't so lucky.

He died before he hit the ground.

Someone called the cops, and when they arrived on the scene Tommy didn't resist arrest. By this time, he had full control of his senses, and was wishing he didn't.

Things would have been easier in a state of blissful ignorance.

Had he been a regular guy, the court might have been lenient. However, being a Navy Seal, the judge seemed determined to make an example of him.

"This society has far too many lawbreakers, Mr. Gardner," the judge said, looking over the rim of his glasses to glare at Tommy sitting with his defense lawyer. "Our children need heroes to look up to. You should be such a hero. Your exploits are commendable. However, you blatantly used your skills to take the life of another person."

The judge shook his head with disgust.

Tommy lowered his gaze to the floor. He knew what was coming and prepared for it. But nothing could have prepared him for the severity of it.

Thirty years to life.

In that moment, Tommy lost everything he'd worked so hard for; his career, his freedom, and his good name. And he had only himself and a moment of bitterness and rage to blame.

Chapter Four

"Gonna catch a square tonight, Navy?" The tall man covered in tattoos asked Tommy. The sun was shining and if Tommy closed his eyes he could almost believe he was a free man.

However, here he stood in the prison yard, convicted of voluntary manslaughter, surrounded with the kind of men he'd built a career trying to put away in prison. Who knew that drinking binge with his brothers three years earlier would lead him down this destructive path?

"Who's the other guy?" Tommy asked in response to the question. When he'd first entered the prison system, he'd proven himself to be someone not easily bullied. With his background in martial arts and street fighting, not many of the other convicts wanted to tangle with him.

"Scruff," the taller man said, pointing to Tommy's would-be opponent.

The man with the shaggy beard stared unblinking at Tommy from across the prison yard. Rumor was he'd murdered his entire family—parents, siblings, and a four year old niece—meticulously, methodically with a hunting knife. The guy was one hundred-proof psychopathic who should have been sedated on the psych ward. Unfortunately, there he stood looking for an opportunity to kill again.

Tommy didn't so much as raise an eyebrow.

The ultimate fights were arranged by Hades, but it was a little known fact that some of the dirty prison guards supported their illegal activities. They were the ones who set up the room without cameras, or supervision. And the survivor's prize was a contraband cell phone.

Tommy had his suspicions why he'd been chosen to fight Scruff. It was common knowledge some of the prison guards were afraid of Scruff and his unpredictable moods. With him gone, they'd have more control.

And Tommy had his own personal reasons to fight. He'd put a couple of Tommy's friends in the prison hospital when they'd fought him. Despite his Seal training, Tommy felt unhinged for a moment at the idea of facing Scruff in combat. The guy who looked like he never washed, fought like a demon from a horror film; no matter how much physical damage he sustained, he kept attacking.

It was as if he didn't feel pain.

"Guess you'd better go put your name on the bill," the man with tattoos said, his grin evil. "Wouldn't want you to miss out on a golden opportunity like this."

Tommy nodded, suspicion knotting his stomach. He needed to ask Hades what Scruff was up to.

Hades was the closest thing to a friend Tommy had in prison. The taller, heavier man had made enough enemies to need someone to watch his back and Tommy fit the bill. Was Scruff trying to eliminate every one in close contact with Haden, a.k.a. Hades?

"Yeah, the fight's on," Hades confirmed when Tommy asked about it. "But you weren't scheduled to be there."

"Then why is that the message I got?"

"Seems to me there might be someone gunning for you in here."

"That's what I figured." Tommy rubbed his elbow. "But now that the word is out I'm going to face Scruff this evening, I might as well go ahead and get it over with. It was due."

"Yeah." Hades didn't contradict him. They both knew what happened to guys who chickened out. They were the ones jumped when they least expected an attack. And if they survived that time, they wouldn't be so lucky again.

Later that night, Tommy and Hades made their way to the secret room designated for the fight. A handful of prisoners waited for them there. There were no rules here. Someone would die. Tommy was confident in his fighting skills, but facing someone like Scruff—someone who could ignore their own pain—the fight could go either way.

After the usual preliminary insults, sneers, and grandstanding from Scruff and his cohorts, Hades whispered last minute encouragement to Tommy.

"Aim for the face," the larger man suggested. "He fights like a demon, but he's got a glass chin."

Tommy nodded his thanks before he turned back to his wild-eyed opponent. A moment later, Hades signaled for the fight to begin. Scruff moved in like a feral dog on a raw steak. He raised both his fists and would have pounded Tommy's back, but Tommy cut him to the floor. Tommy nearly had Scruff in a submission-style hold, but the squirming man managed to get away with frightening ease.

Tommy smashed Scruff's nose with his elbow. Blood splattered everything within a six-foot radius. Tommy rolled out of reach. Scruff didn't so much as blink at the blood running down his chin.

He rushed forward again.

Tommy waited for the opening, and saw it when Scruff swung wide like a demented windmill. He focused his final punch on Scruff's still bleeding nose.

Game over.

Scruff hit the floor and didn't move again. His body was left in a heap like day old garbage. One of the corrupt guards would doctor the papers to make it appear like a suicide, which was their usual practice.

Hailed a hero, Tommy had an uncomfortable feeling drizzle down his spine. Something was wrong, very wrong. Someone had gone to a lot of trouble to set up this fight.

"Don't let your guard down," Hades said after Tommy confided in him his concerns. "You could be right."

Over the next few weeks, nothing happened. Tommy relaxed a little. He and Hades even managed to joke about visiting the prison chaplain.

"You should go," Hades said one afternoon as they milled outside in the exercise yard. "Even just to get a break from the regular riff raff."

"Naw, that religion stuff isn't for me."

"Who said anything about religion? It gets me out of here for a while." He sent a glare at a rival gang standing across the yard from them, who were laughing and smoking cigarettes.

"It'd do you the world of good."

"I don't know." Tommy shrugged, tossing his nearly finished cigarette to the ground and dug his heel into it.

"It could mean early parole," Hades said.

"Look at me, man." Tommy gave Hades a frank look. "I'm a convicted killer. With my background, no one is going to give me a second chance at society."

"That's where you're wrong." Hades leaned in closer and lowered his voice. "With a little acting, you could fool the chaplain."

"Like you?" Tommy quirked his eyebrow in open cynicism and smiled humorlessly. "Sorry, it ain't gonna happen." The temperature was rising, and he wiped the sweat off his brow with the back of his sleeve. "Besides, I'm not into acting like I'm anything other than what I am. What you see is what you get: Navy Seal serving time for murder. End of story."

"Then you'd rather rot in prison." Hades glowered at his friend. "Hey buddy, your choice. It's not gonna be mine."

Tommy didn't watch Hades leave, his attention was on the guys across the yard. He'd caught a few of their glances, seen anger brewing there, and wondered when they'd strike next.

What he wouldn't give for a break from the violence and rising tension. In a way, Tommy wished he could pretend to be something he wasn't if only for the sake of early release, but it went against every bit of his Seal training. His integrity was worth far more to him than freedom.

Too bad.

However, a man's integrity meant nothing in prison if someone wanted him dead.

The next day, while leaving the laundry facility where he worked, the sound of angry voices rushed up from the most dangerous area of the prison. Alarms sounded, and the voice of a guard came over the sound system, urging prisoners to return to their cells.

While sprinting towards his cell, he spied Hades being led back down the hall in handcuffs. Nothing out of the ordinary there. Hades always returned from the chaplain's office in cuffs.

He watched as the guard left the big man unattended to help the other guards stop the escalating riot. That left Hades unprotected. And Tommy wasn't the only one who noticed.

One of his rival gang members had cornered Hades.

Tommy started running towards his friend when he noticed another man, carrying a shank, heading in Hades' direction. From the glint in the prisoner's narrowed eyes, it was easy to tell he intended to use the makeshift weapon on Hades.

He shouted out a warning, but it was swallowed up by the chaos in the prison; shouts of rage and pain, and orders snapped out by the guards. It was the kind of thing to strike fear in any man's heart.

He didn't make it in time. Hades fell under the attack. Tommy turned towards his cell but someone else with a shank knifed him in the stomach. While his life flowed from the wound, Tommy looked up into the face of his killer.

"You should be dead already, Navy," the man shouted. "It's why I went to all the trouble to set up that fight between you and Scruff."

Tommy couldn't catch his breath. He managed to glance around him, that's when he knew no one would notice him out there bleeding to death.

"Goodbye, Navy." His killer stepped over Tommy's struggling body. "No one will remember you by the end of the day."

The first thing Tommy saw when his eyes opened were the pristine white ceiling.

He should be dead; he knew. But the distinct smell of disinfectant told him otherwise. He swallowed and winced at the pain. He lifted his hand and felt the bandage on his stomach. Cautiously, he glanced around him, without turning his head, and noticed the I.V. pole next to his bed. His gaze followed the tubing down to where it was taped to the back of his hand.

He'd never been in the hospital infirmary before but it didn't take a genius to recognize his whereabouts. How long had it been since the prison riot; he wondered. And how long since he'd been unconscious?

The questions were forgotten when Hades screamed. Tommy tried to push the blankets off him but didn't have the strength. The very act of raising his head brought a gasp of intense pain.

"It's real! I saw it! Hell is real!"

Hades' voice sliced the silence as effectively as the shank blade had cut Tommy's stomach muscles. Tommy had no way of knowing what was going on. The curtain between the beds was closed.

Tommy clenched his hands into fists. The terror in the other man's voice was tangible, and he was helpless to find out what was going on. But his friend was alive, and that was enough for him.

"Its okay, Haden," another man spoke in soothing tones from the other side of the closed curtain. "You're in the infirmary."

"I saw Hell. It's real. God, save me, it's real!"

Hades had to be hallucinating. Tommy thought to himself, pressing his fist to his forehead. The only Hell that existed was the one people put you through. Surely there couldn't be any more punishment waiting after all the pain people endured in this life?

Tommy couldn't help but hear the chaplain reassure Hades he was still alive. But what convinced Tommy his friend wasn't playing a game was when he begged the chaplain to read some Bible to him.

Bible. Tommy sneered. What he needed to do was plot how to get rid of the guys who'd tried to kill him and Hades. The only Bible that guy would hear, would be at his funeral.

Tommy tried to ignore what was being read out loud, but the words slipped past his anger and thoughts of revenge.

Could a merciful God forgive him for all the things he'd done? Tommy laughed scoffed at his weakening thoughts, and turned his back on the closed curtain.

After weeks of recovery, Tommy no longer experienced pain. However, Hades took longer. While he remained in the infirmary, Hades rambled on at various times about when he was a kid going to Sunday school and about God.

The first time Tommy heard Hades sing 'Jesus loves me', he nearly fell out of bed.

"Yes, Haden. Jesus does love you."

During his stay in the infirmary, Tommy recognized the chaplain's voice.

"Do I have hope?" Hades demanded to know, nearly hysterical as he grabbed the chaplain's arm and stared up at him.

"Yes, there is hope for anyone willing to repent of their sins."

It didn't take long for Tommy to grow tired of hearing the same conversation between the other men. He'd long given up hope and didn't want to hear anyone talk about anything remotely encouraging. He was a murderer. It didn't matter that Hades was too, Tommy had no excuse. His training should have kept him from taking the life of a civilian.

Nope, he turned his face to the wall; there was no hope for Tommy Gardner. He had other things on his mind, like evening the score with the guy who'd knifed him.

However, within an hour of his release back to his cell, Tommy learned that the men who had started the riot had been transferred to another maximum prison, and that included the guy who'd plunged the knife into his gut.

It was also leaked to the press about the ultimate fighting events that occurred within the prison, and an investigation was launched. In an effort to sweep the evidence away, Tommy and Hades were both transferred out of there hours before the investigation started. However, he wasn't sent to the same prison as his friend.

He'd barely settled into his cell when he was called before the parole board.

"Special Warfare Operator 1st Class Petty Officer Thomas Gardner," the woman in the center of the parole board acknowledged him by his full Navy Seal title, something he hadn't heard in what seemed like a hundred years.

"Yes, Ma'am." He stood to attention, every inch a Navy Seal as if he'd stood before them in uniform.

"It has reached our attention," she began in a no-nonsense voice, the kind he was used to, "that you have proven yourself an ideal prisoner. You have followed the rules to the letter. In light of the investigation into the last penitentiary where you were held for the past three years, the guards who have not been indicted on charges of criminal activity have written to us encouraging us to let you be paroled.

"Well, Mr. Gardner, what do you have to say?"

Tommy's chin rose an inch higher, realizing he had to give the most compelling speech of his life if he was to gain his freedom. And he did.

"I would rather be on the firing line, saving my country, Ma'am, than living as one of the men I vowed to put behind bars."

That day, Tommy was paroled.

However, he found out later from reading the newspaper, the real reason for his early parole was on account of the illegal fighting in prison. He had grounds for suing the system. But being tied up for years in the court system didn't interest Tommy.

He'd been given the gift of life. Again. And he didn't plan on squandering it. Again.

Chapter Five

In his eagerness to start living again, he never considered important things, like finding a job. His naval career was over. Potential employers didn't want to give him a chance when they found out about his prison record.

Life does come full circle, he thought as he sat at the table in his half-way house during dinner. The other men who shared the house ignored him. And that suited Tommy. He wasn't looking for a fight. He'd had enough of those in prison.

However, if he didn't find stability soon, a way to support himself, he'd end up homeless, out on the street, scrounging food from garbage cans and keeping warm with newspapers. The thought made him uneasy.

What did guys like him do to find employment?

"The job prospects aren't good," one of the counselors in the half-way house told him. "Unfortunately they're worse for someone with your background in this job market."

Tommy didn't need to hear that, but he had to face facts sooner or later.

"I don't want to live off government aid," Tommy said in a near growl. "I've had a career." He'd had a home, a car, and self-respect. Now he had none of those things. Failure loomed before his eyes. All because of one fatal mistake, everything he'd worked hard for had been taken from him.

However, his parole officer had better news for Tommy by the end of his first week on parole.

"The local oil refinery is hiring," the man said. "Might want to get a resume over there ASAP. You can even use me as a reference."

Tommy had a resume into the office by the end of the day. Within twenty four hours, he'd been hired, effective the following morning.

His first day of the job should have been a good one. However, he met up with his past in the form of another guy from his gang. A guy who'd been released before Tommy was paroled.

"How's it goin', Navy?"

"Stone." Tommy shook the other man's outstretched hand. He hoped his history wouldn't spread around his new job site.

As if sensing Tommy's dilemma, Stone grinned. "So, new guy, huh? What do you think of this place?"

"Seems ok."

Anyone watching them would think they were engaged in small talk, but paroled convicts didn't discuss things like the weather and feelings. Stone, a known drug runner, wouldn't mind jeopardizing Tommy's newfound employment if it meant getting him what he wanted. It didn't take long for Tommy to discover just exactly what Stone wanted.

"Fish is out," Stone said. "You remember Fish, don't you, Navy?"'

"Yeah." Tommy crossed his arms over his chest, sniffed, and made sure no one could over hear them.

"He's got a market on the corner."

Translation: Fish was pushing drugs again.

"Good for him." Tommy nodded.

"He's got more work than I can handle." Stone flashed him a smile, the kind Tommy wanted to plow his fist into. "I think he'd like it if you went round to help him out."

"Yeah, sure." Tommy flexed his shoulders in a shrug. He wasn't interested in what Fish was up to, but if he intended to keep his co-workers out of his business he might just have to bend on this. But he wasn't going to let Stone push him too far. Even if it meant quitting.

Stone gave him an address before he sauntered down the hall.

After work, Tommy didn't feel like returning to the half-way house immediately. As long as he was back before dark he'd be okay. That meant he had a little over an hour to relax. He chose a nearby restaurant. His plans included coffee, a donut, and the day's newspaper.

His plans didn't unfold as he'd hoped. It just so happened that the restaurant he chose belonged to Stone's friend, Fish.

"Hey, it's Navy," Fish called out a warm greeting, getting up from where he sat at a table with a group of men wearing expensive suits and stern expressions.

The temptation to leave sent Tommy rocking back on his heels.

"Come here." Fish waved him over. The reason he'd been nicknamed fish was on account of his being wall-eyed, with a long face and a large mouth.

With a great deal of reluctance, Tommy moved forward to shake hands with yet another bad memory from his past. "These are my associates," Fish said, and made introductions. Tommy nodded at each one glancing quickly at them and away. People of this ilk didn't like being stared at.

"Sit down, sit down." Fish reached over and pulled a chair out for him. The atmosphere was civil with undercurrents of danger. Something not quite above board was going on here and Tommy wished to be a million miles away.

"I ran into Stone," Tommy said, figuring he'd better get the information out in the open. "Said you might have some work."

"Did he?" Fish laughed. "Good man, Stone. He's right. I have some furniture that needs moving."

Tommy swallowed his sigh of protest. He'd hoped Fish wouldn't have anything for him.

"Tell you what," Fish said, "Go sit at the table over by the cash register and when I'm done talking to these gentlemen we can discuss a few details. Order whatever you want, it's on the house."

"Sure." Tommy glanced at his watch. "But I can only stay for another forty five minutes. I'm due back at my half-way house."

"Not a problem." Fish waved him off, turning his attention back to the other men at his table.

Alone at the table, and cursing his bad luck, Tommy sat down and picked up the day's crumpled news paper; the original reason he was there in the first place.

"Hi."

Tommy glanced up at the kind voice and scowled. Standing beside him was a pink-cheeked waitress holding a tray with food.

"I hope you don't mind if I sit here," she said, as if unaware of the darkening scowl on his face. "I'm on my break and this is the unofficial break table."

"Help yourself." He moved the newspaper to accommodate her tray and then returned his attention to the article he'd been reading.

"They call it news," she said, unwrapping her chicken sandwich, "but I find it ironic, given the fact they rehash the same stories for weeks on end."

She was a talker, Tommy nearly groaned. The day just got better and better. At least she was pretty, in a blonde-blue-eyed girl next door kind of way. He continued to read without acknowledging her comment.

"Lord, thank You, for this food."

Tommy's gaze jumped from the page to the waitress' closed eyes and bowed head.

"Bless it to give me the energy I need for today," she said, as if unaware of him staring at her, "and bless the man sitting at this table with me. Amen."

Tommy blinked, dumbfounded. If he wasn't waiting for a drug lord to discuss business with, he'd have been back at the half-way house by now.

"Why'd you do that?" he asked before he could stop himself. When she looked up at him and raised an eyebrow, he hurried to explain what he meant. "Why'd you pray for me?"

It had been the oddest experience of his life. His mother never once taught him how to say prayers, and hearing someone else talk to God on his behalf was as foreign to him as learning to knit socks.

"Because you're a human being," she told him before biting into her sandwich. "And I like to pray for people."

He continued to watch her, unable to help it. His life had been about brutality, first in his home, then his job, and then prison. This small woman with her courteous smiles and twinkling eyes was something he'd never come into contact with before. It left him feeling oddly off kilter much like the first time he stood on deck of a speeding boat.

"I'm Becca," she said. "And you are?"

Tommy opened his mouth to respond, but then didn't exactly know how to. Did he give her his former Navy Seal title?

Or his prison number? Should he tell her he was a parolee living at a half-way house with a horrible past, a dark present, and a bleak future?

"Tommy Gardner." He decided on the name he'd written on his resume. Simple Mister nobody-worth-crying-over-Tommy-Gardner.

"Nice to meet you," she said. "I'm the cook here, so if the food doesn't taste right go see a doctor."

His eyebrows rose slightly.

"I'm kidding." Becca shook her head. "Ugh, I can see you're one of those."

"One of what?" He didn't mean to be sharp, but it'd been a long time since someone had teased him.

"One of those people who don't have a sense of humor."

Was she for real? Tommy frowned again. Didn't she realize the type of business that went on under the roof where she worked?

"Why are you sitting here talking to me?" he asked her bluntly. "You don't know what I'm doing here, reading this paper and waiting for your boss."

"Sure I do. You're probably going to work for the big boss." She nodded and took another bite. The nonchalance of her reply took his breath away. Was she insane? Any one of the criminals involved with Fish would snuff out her life and step over her dead body without a second thought. "Like move some packages around for him. Or kill someone. Or, I don't know, a million other illegal things my boss corrupts others with."

"Why do you put yourself in danger by being here?"

"For you, Tommy." It was a straight-from-the-hip kind of answer he didn't expect to hear, not from a young woman like Becca. "For you and guys like you who need someone to throw a lifeline to you."

Chapter Six

"You say that," Tommy said, looking away from the concern and genuine caring in her blue eyes, "like you really mean it."

"I do mean it." She set her sandwich aside, and folded her hands together on the table. "My younger brother had the whole world ahead of him."

Great, just what he needed to hear, a sob story. But Tommy's cynicism didn't last as the words flowed from her heart.

"But things never work out the way we think they will," she said, shaking her head slowly. "Colin got hooked on drugs, was robbed a few times, and ended up owing a lot of money to the wrong people. He was terrified they'd catch him. Drug dealers have very little mercy for those they feel wronged them." Tears slipped down her face, she reached for the silver napkin holder, pulled out a couple napkins and dabbed at her damp eyes. "Colin made sure they wouldn't torture him before he died. He took matters into his own hands and hung himself."

"I'm sorry." Tommy said, reaching out and touching her arm in a gesture of compassion, something he didn't think he had anymore. "But why do you continue to work in a place full of garbage like Fish and his gang?"

"When Colin died, I was devastated. I'm a born again believer, Tommy," she glanced up at him as if gauging his reaction to that announcement. "I knew his soul was lost for eternity if he wasn't right with God in those last few moments of his life. I hope he was."

She chewed thoughtfully for a few moments before she continued. "This was the last place I wanted to work in after I found out what was going on, but I felt God telling me to stay;

that He'd bring to me people He planned to help get out of this way of life."

She hadn't answered his question, but he didn't feel like ridiculing her stand on what he classified as religion. He remembered how Hades had changed after he'd come out of his coma. He'd given his life to the One named Jesus. But Tommy didn't want it, not if it weakened him; turning the cheek and all that.

"Your brother wouldn't want you to stay here," Tommy said, hoping he could change her mind about the restaurant's sordid clientele. "He'd want you to get a decent job working for law abiding citizens."

And not talking to dangerous ex-cons like him.

"I promised God," Becca said with a frown. "I told Him that if I could reach just one life, put myself between them and Hell I'd do it. No matter the cost."

Tommy's mouth dropped in a silent 'oh'. He'd never met anyone like this woman. If his mother had been half the person Becca was his father wouldn't have gotten away with his riotous lifestyle. His brothers wouldn't have used him as a punching bag, and he'd never have gone to prison.

"That's why you're sitting here, talking to me like I was a regular Joe," Tommy said, humbled. He dropped his gaze to the salt and pepper shakers in the middle of the table.

"You're important, Tommy," she told him. "You have far more value than you know."

"It's too late for me," he said, putting into words what he wouldn't have confessed an hour earlier. "I've done things."

"That's why Jesus died on the cross for all the world," she said, "A world that hated Him. He died for you Tommy, because He knows you're worth saving."

Tommy didn't respond but something in his heart throbbed. Could it be true? Could God really not be finished with him?

"My church is having a concert this week," she said, her words coming out in a hurry as if her time had expired. "Here's the flyer." Becca pushed a bookmark sized flyer in his direction before they were interrupted.

"Isn't your break over, Becca?" Fish asked in a voice that didn't leave room for argument.

"Yes, I guess it is." She stood up, taking her tray with her. "Consider what we talked about, Tommy," she said, her eyes pleading with him before she disappeared into the kitchen.

"That one," Fish said, shaking his head as if aggravated. "If she wasn't the best cook for miles she'd be on the unemployment line."

Tommy didn't say anything. Instead, he tucked the concert flyer in his shirt pocket and watched as Fish sat down in Becca's vacated chair.

"Shall we get down to business?" The evil glint in Fish's wall-eyed gaze was vastly different from the glow in the cook's.

That night, Tommy lay in bed, his arms under his head as he tried to focus on what Fish expected of him. The drug dealer had set everything up for Friday night. Yet Tommy couldn't get Becca's words out of his head.

Could she be right? Could God truly love him? Was it possible that there might be more to life than he thought? Tommy hoped so. He really, truly hoped so.

The rest of the week zoomed by. Only because he didn't want Friday to arrive, Tommy thought, as he stood looking in the bathroom mirror while he ran the razor over his jaw. It wasn't a prison issued disposable razor, but one he'd bought with his own money; a huge thing to someone with his history.

Was he willing to sacrifice even that little freedom? He wondered. Was it worth getting caught and being sent back to prison for the sake of having people at his work place find out about his past?

Tommy set aside the razor and gripped the sides of the sink.

"God," it was his first attempt at prayer and the words were difficult to say but they came from his heart, "Please, don't let me do this. If You honestly care...for me...don't let me get mixed up with this scene."

A sense of peace, the kind Tommy never felt before in his life, calmed his mind. After showering and dressing in clean jeans and a blue tee shirt, Tommy went ahead and followed through with Fish's instructions that he'd given him at the restaurant.

However, Tommy had a few minutes before he was to meet his contact, so he decided to go to the grocery store, if for nothing else, to take in some of the shopping atmosphere. Prison separated people from doing things the average person had the freedom to experience every day.

"Hey, you!"

Tommy knew that voice. He looked around and saw Becca grinning at him from where she stood in the fresh produce section.

"Hi." He rubbed the back of his neck, suddenly nervous. "What brings you here?"

"Apple pie," she said simply, holding up a bag of Cortlands to prove her point. "Or rather apples to make the pie."

How long had it been since he'd had homemade pie?

"What about you?" She smiled, raising a blonde eyebrow at him. "This doesn't seem like the kind of place you'd like to hang out at."

It wasn't, but he didn't want her to think he was anything but normal. He certainly couldn't explain that he was killing time.

"I needed a pack of gum," he said.

"Oh." She carefully placed her selected apples into the hand basket hanging from her arm. "So, did you give it any more thought, the concert, I mean?"

"Um, yeah." He didn't want to commit to anything when he didn't know where he'd be that night. If the cops picked him up, he'd be back behind bars for parole violation and trafficking drugs. And the last thing he wanted to do was disappoint Becca.

"I hope you decided to go." The anticipate in her eyes made him wish he'd met her before his life had taken the wrong turn.

"I'm not sure just yet," he said. "It depends on how my day goes."

"Be careful, Tommy," she said, moving close enough to put her cool hand on his bare arm. The sincerity in her eyes warmed his heart; and made him ashamed. "I don't want anything bad to happen to you."

"Could you keep me in your prayers, today?" he asked, suddenly finding it difficult to breathe. "I won't expect you to do that again, but just for today."

"It'd be an honor," she assured him, her smile widened. "I've prayed for you since we talked in the restaurant the other day. In fact, I want you to have this." She reached into her purse and pulled out a small Bible.

"Thank you." He accepted the Bible, touching it as if it was made of solid gold. He lowered his head, humbled that someone as warm and lovely as Becca even remembered his name. "I...I got to go now."

"Good bye, Tommy," she said. "And God bless you."

Tommy sat on the corner of the street in an old beat up station wagon that evening as the sky darkened with the night. Fish arranged for a car to be there for him since he didn't own one. The hunk of junk of a car would keep the cops off his back while he waited for his contact to pick up the parcel. How God could give him peace while he was about to break even more laws Tommy didn't know but after meeting Becca at the grocery store, he wasn't about to question God's plans. He touched the Bible in his shirt pocket and grinned. Maybe things weren't as bleak as he thought they were.

Unexpectedly, a police car pulled up and parked behind the station wagon. Tommy straightened up in his seat, his heart hammering at his larynx. If he could talk sensibly in the next five seconds he just might be able to stay out of jail.

But maybe he'd been deluding himself with hope. Tommy's eyes slid shut with defeat. Did God plan to toss him back into that jungle? And if he was, it was nothing less than he deserved.

Chapter Seven

"Well, praise God, brother," the police officer said when he looked through the rolled down window. Tommy jumped when the officer's arm shot out to shake his hand. "It's about time someone tried to evangelize this neighborhood."

"Uh, yeah." Not sure how to respond to that, Tommy let the other man pump his arm. What in the world made the officer think he was a preacher?

"Your bumper stickers are sure to make people think. Keep up the good work," the officer said turning on his heel to return to his own car. "And God bless you."

It was the second time that day someone said that to him, Tommy realized, amazed. Could it be that God was truly leading him even as he was breaking the law by having illegal goods in the car?

The mention of a bumper sticker piqued his curiosity. Tommy opened the door and got out of the car with the intent of seeing it for himself. He chuckled when he read, *Don't Let The Car Fool You, My Real Treasure Is In Heaven.* And *This Car Is Prayer Conditioned.* But the one that made him think said; *The Road To Integrity Is Always Under Construction.*

When he returned to the driver's seat, he couldn't help thinking about the meaning behind what had happened. Was Becca right? That God wanted to show him better things? Tommy hoped so because he didn't want to end up working for guys like Fish until he died.

When it became clear that his contact wasn't going to show up after three hours of waiting, Tommy returned to the half-way house. He despised carrying the parcel with him, but he didn't dare leave it in the car. It felt like a leaden weight in his arm, but what else could he do? If he didn't do what Fish expected, he'd be in big trouble, the kind that involved cement shoes and the local river.

That night, his contact called.

"I saw that cop talking to you," the gravelly voiced man said. "I can't take the chance of getting caught. We'll try it again tomorrow."

After receiving another drop off location, Tommy hung up the phone feeling even worse. Was it never going to end?

As Tommy went to get into the car the following afternoon, he paused at the rear bumper. He read the stickers again and grinned.

Suddenly, the weight on Tommy's shoulders eased off. Everything truly was going to be okay, he just knew it.

However, as Tommy drove to the next allotted spot to meet his contact, two squad cars pulled into traffic immediately behind him.

Sweat broke out on Tommy's forehead. Not all police officers were Christians, that much he knew from experience. Chances were slim these two would care whether he had a Christian bumper sticker or not. If they followed him to the drop off point, they'd know what he was up to for sure.

"God, help me," he prayed for the second time in his life.

As he continued to worry how he was going to handle the situation, he noticed a large parking lot filled with vehicles, and in the middle was what looked to be a circus tent. Tommy signaled a right turn, figuring he'd hide out there.

The cops followed him into the parking lot.

This was it. They knew. Tommy regained his composure when they didn't flash the lights of the police car at him. He opened the car door and got out.

One of the officers he recognized from the day before; the one who'd commended him for his religious work in the neighborhood.

"Well, praise God, brother," the officer called out in greeting as he and the other cop made their way towards the tent.

"Tonight is going to be something else. The best gospel music and the best speakers. Better hurry, or all the good seats will be gone."

Tommy's jaw slackened before he forced a grin as he looked at the signs posted around the tent. It was the concert Becca had wanted him to attend.

God cared! He really did care!

"So I heard," he said when he could speak.

He found an empty seat near the back, and felt conspicuous. Would people know his life story by looking at him? What was a guy like him hoping God could do? He'd be better off ending his life than raising false hopes he stood a chance of God's forgiveness.

As the music ended, the speaker was introduced. Tommy shook his head to clear it. Surely, he'd misunderstood. Did they say Haden Lambert was going to preach?

Sure enough, the man Tommy knew as Hades stepped towards the podium. Shock went through him like a bullet. How could this be?

"Let me tell you," Haden said as if he'd heard the unspoken question, looking at the crowd with a huge grin, "How God took someone with little to recommend them as a human being and changed them through the life altering power of the blood of Jesus Christ, His Only Begotten Son."

Haden, formerly known as Hades, told the story of a boy who'd been violently abused as a child, cast off from society when he made a name for himself with his fists, and went on to getting involved in the seediest side of criminal activities.

"And then God, in His infinite mercy and wisdom, allowed me a sneak peak of Hell."

Tommy sat forward in his seat, eager and hungry to hear the outcome of what he already knew to be fact.

"It changed my life. I stopped denying God's existence, and asked Him instead to live within me. And He did." Haden's voice broke with emotion. "When I gave my life to Him, He made a new person of me, gave me a reason for living, and gave me a future. My friend," Haden took the microphone and walked to the edge of the stage, "If you're here and you have a past you're ashamed of, and a future without hope, you've come to the right place. Jesus Christ can take the hopelessness out of your life and fill it with His presence. You will discover a peace you've never thought possible."

To hear the former tough man who bragged he had no conscience tell his story made it clear to Tommy that he did indeed have hope. The Holy Spirit convicted Tommy of the wrongs in his past; that he was to blame for the choices that sent him to prison, and that the choice to be free was now within his grasp. All he had to do was ask God for forgiveness through the saving blood His Son, Jesus Christ, shed on the cross for him.

It was the quickest and best decision Tommy ever made in his life.

As Tommy stood at the altar with the other people who wanted salvation, he knew the moment Haden recognized him. He could see the shock and joy wash over the other man's face before he pressed through the crowd to him.

"I thought you were dead," Haden said, grabbing Tommy by the shoulders. "I tried to find out what happened but no one could tell me anything."

Not sure what to say to that, Tommy remained silent.

"Praise God for getting you here this evening," Haden said, tears flowing freely from his eyes. "Come with me. You've got to meet some people."

Before Tommy knew it, Haden put his arm around his shoulders and led him towards a gathering of the people that had been with Haden on the platform, including the police officers that had followed Tommy into the tent. Suddenly shy, Tommy tried to hang back but Haden wouldn't let him.

"You're family now, brother," he said.

Tommy wasn't just treated like family, they acted like he was long lost royalty. The friends he'd made that evening let him know he was just as important as anyone else, despite his past. And someone was quick to tell him that giving his life over to Jesus made him a brand new person. The man formerly known as Tommy the ex-con was gone, and in his place stood Tommy the born again believer.

"You made it!"

The sweetest voice Tommy knew spoke at his side. He turned and saw Becca's face, her smile let him know just how happy his presence there made her.

"I nearly didn't," he admitted, feeling awkward and shy.

"I prayed and God gave me my heart's desire." She laughed and squeezed his arm.

Tears clogged Tommy's throat. He hadn't cried since he was a kid when he'd vowed no one would ever hurt him again. However, this time he didn't cry from pain but rather from the joy that filled his now clean heart. He did indeed feel like a new man. But he did have one more thing to do before he could settle into his new life.

"—And I'm not working for you anymore," he said into the telephone the minute he got back to the half-way house.

"She got to you, didn't she?" Fish's voice sounded oddly resigned. "Becca has that effect on people."

"God did," Tommy clarified. "And I'm never going back to that kind of life again."

"And he never did," Mike said, as Faith and Jane cleared away the supper dishes.

"What happened to Becca?" Jane asked, scraping the remains from one plate into the garbage.

"She married Tommy." Mike grinned. "They got a kid now, and you'd never know that former Navy Seal slash ex-con had it in him to get on his hands and knees and carry his son on his back, horse-style."

"Do you have any more stories?" Jane asked.

"Tell her about the guy who lived under water for days," Faith suggested.

"Yes," Jane said. "Tell me that one."

"Well, technically, he didn't live under water," Mike clarified, chuckling. "But he did have an extended stay in the stuff."

Father Went Missing

Chapter One

Wayne Young stepped inside the church foyer. It was empty, just like the parking lot that Monday afternoon. Exactly what he'd hoped for. He turned his gaze to the door marked as the pastor's study, and headed there.

"It's open," Pastor Haden said on the first knock.

Wayne opened the door.

"Come in, Wayne," the pastor invited. "I've been waiting for you."

The older man stepped into the study, took one of the empty chairs and deflated like a balloon. His head sank to his chest and his back bowed. "I…I'm going to kill myself today, Pastor."

Pastor Haden didn't react to the unpleasant declaration other than to step around his desk and take the seat next to his afternoon visitor.

"Why is that an option?"

"If I don't, the mob will." Wayne shook his head. "They'll go after my family, everyone I care about, until I'm gone."

"What makes you think they'll do that?"

"Because…I heard things I wasn't supposed to," Wayne said. "I heard plans they were planning to bomb their rival's warehouse. I've told the police about it, but there's nothing they can do."

"God can make a way out of this situation," Pastor Haden said, resting his hand on the other man's slumped shoulder. "All you need to do is give the situation over to Him."

"You make it sound so easy." Wayne shook his head without looking up. "Like prayer is magical."

"Far from magic." Pastor Haden chuckled. "There is nothing mightier than God, and when He intervenes on behalf of His children, no one can stand in the way. Not the mob, not the most hardened criminal, and not the government. I should know; I used to be a prisoner. But when I gave my life over to God, He made things happen that I wouldn't have believed possible if I hadn't seen them with my own eyes."

"I'd rather trust God…" he took a deep breath, his shoulders rising and falling beneath his expensive business jacket, "…than put a bullet through my brain."

"That's right, you would." The pastor stepped back and reached for his Bible opened on his desk. "There are many people, men and women, who went through crisis thinking they had no way out. But then God intervened on their behalf, and things changed."

"Yeah?" Wayne's brown eyes filled with hope as he raised his face to look at the pastor. "Like who?"

"Well, King David for example," the pastor said, flipping through a few pages in his Bible. "He was the king of Israel and yet he was hounded day and night by a jealous Saul, David's own father-in-law. Saul wanted to destroy David. He and his men tracked him constantly, and yet time after time God saved King David from death."

"Sounds like what I'm going through now," Wayne said.

"And David, at his most depressed moments, wrote songs to God, begging for help. Which God always provided. And at one point David comes to the realization of God's saving power when he wrote, "where can I flee from your presence, if I go up to the heavens you are there, if I make my bed in the depths you are there."

"You make a convincing argument, Pastor."

"Why don't we pray about this situation?"

Together the two men brought Wayne's problem to the Lord, and when they were finished Wayne had surrendered his life to God.

"Go home and spend some time with your family," Pastor Haden said.

"I can't." Wayne felt ashamed by that admission. "Me and the boys haven't spent time together since they were kids."

"What did you do together when they were youngsters?"

"Camp."

"Then why don't you round up your people and go?" the pastor suggested. "The church has a couple vans stocked with camping gear. They're used mainly for traveling ministry, but no one's booked them for the next few weeks. You're more than welcome to use one of them."

"You know, I'm going to take you up on that offer," Wayne said, smiling for the first time in months. "First I'll call the kids, and then I'll be back to get the van." He stood up and held out his hand. "Thank you, Pastor. You're a life saver."

Once out in his Cadillac, Wayne called his oldest son on his cell phone.

"Yeah, I want to go fishing," his sixteen year old son, Blake, said enthusiastically. "You're really going to take the time off work?"

"It's been ten years since I took a break," Wayne said, feeling fresh tears well up in his eyes. "I think I'm due."

"I'll say," Blake agreed. "I'll go tell Mom and Kev. Oh man, I can't wait."

The details were settled, and two days later Wayne showed up at the church to get the van. He left his Cadillac in the parking lot, handed the keys to the pastor and told him to enjoy the car.

"You know," Pastor Haden said, jingling the keys in his hand, "I just might like driving the Cadillac for a while. But on the other hand," he flashed a mischievous grin at Wayne. "I don't want the flesh to get too comfortable, so I'll stick with my old faithful puddle jumper."

"Your choice," Wayne joked, knowing he wouldn't trust anyone else with his new car besides the pastor. It didn't matter what kind of sordid things Pastor Haden had done in the past, he was a new man and every decision he made now reflected the change that God had done in his life.

He was truly a marvel.

"Any word about that thing we'd talked about the other day?" the pastor asked, cautious with the way he broached the subject.

"You've seen the news, haven't you?" Wayne asked. "They went ahead and blew up the warehouse. No one is taking responsibility, but you and I both know who's to blame. The police asked me questions, but I didn't have enough information for them."

"Get away for a while," the pastor said. "I'll park your car in my garage, no one will see it there."

"Thank you, Pastor," Wayne said, grateful to have found a friend as trustworthy as the Pastor. He turned to go but then turned back. "I should mention one thing." Wayne gritted his teeth, wondering how he could say it without making it sound worse than it was. "When I got into business, I hadn't realized just how close to the mob I'd be. I've never wanted anything to do with them, but it seems I can't get away from their dealings."

"I will put that on the prayer list too," the pastor said. "God can make a way where there seems to be no way. Go in the safety and peace of our Lord Jesus Christ."

Wayne felt better knowing Pastor Haden didn't condemn him for what he'd told him. As he drove the van away, he had high hopes for the few days he'd spend with his family. God would take care of the rest.

Chapter Two

Officer David Emerson got the missing person's report early that afternoon. He read the facts and grunted. Nothing unusual: man suspected of being in the mob disappears, and no one has heard from him in over three days. Likely he'd ended up dead and buried where he wouldn't be found for a hundred years.

What he didn't like was that he knew the man listed as missing.

Wayne Young.

Just the other day Pastor Haden told him about Wayne Young and his visit to his church office. That was Monday, today was Friday. Each day that passed, Wayne's chances for survival—if he was alive—diminished significantly.

He didn't relish telling Young's family, particularly the boys, Kev and Blake, about their father. He'd known them since they were kids. They'd been involved in the local chapter of Scouts where David volunteered his time, and then when they started attending Sunday school services at his church. Gwen, Wayne's wife, was a wonderful person who never gave up praying for her husband to get saved.

There'd been a lot of rejoicing when Wayne finally gave in to the Lord. The Lord had begun a reconciliation work between him and his family, beginning with the family camping trip. But something happened to cut those plans before they happened, and it was up to him to find out what.

Why go to the trouble of borrowing the church's camping gear and van if he didn't intend to use them?

Perhaps to throw off the mob; it sounded likely, a possibility David had to consider as a police officer. But it didn't gel, not after hearing the pastor give his account of the events leading up to the moment Wayne left the parking lot with the van.

"I knew it seemed too good to be true." Gwen cried into her hands when the pastor and David visited her and the boys that evening. The pastor and David's father, Harry Senior, and two other men from the church board surrounded her while they prayed for Wayne's safe keeping and for God to reveal where he was.

Dead or alive. But that remained unspoken.

The boys weren't as moderate in their grief. "So they caught up with Dad!" Twelve year old Kev had the look of a thundercloud in his face. "The kids at school said he was bought and owned by the mob, but I didn't believe it."

"Kevin," his mother said, her tone both a reprimand and plea. "Don't make this more difficult than it already is."

"I hope he's dead," Kev continued to rage, tears flooding his eyes. "I'm tired of his lies! He never does anything he says he's going to do!"

David caught Kevin when the boy raced for the door. He picked him up around the waist and hugged him even as his thin arms and legs kicked out at him.

"It's okay to be mad, Kev," David said in a kind voice that he'd used on many distraught kids.

"I didn't mean it." The boy's emotional storm broke and Kev clung to the officer, letting his tears flow free. "I didn't mean it."

"Of course you didn't," David agreed, smoothing the boy's hair down. "These next couple days might be difficult, and you need to be strong for your mom. Can you do that?"

"Yeah." Kev's head moved slightly against David's shoulder.

"Good." David released him. "Now go tell your mom you're sorry."

"I'm sorry, Mom." Kev rubbed at his eyes with the back of his sleeve as he stood beside his mother. She took his free hand and smiled up at him through her own tears.

"He's coming back, Kevin," she said, reassuring her youngest son. "Dad will be home soon."

Kev nodded, keeping his eyes downcast. For their sakes, David hoped what she said would be fact and not just wishful thinking. He'd seen enough during his stint as an officer to know the mob didn't play games, they didn't give second chances, and if they wanted someone dead accidents were easily arranged.

"If you need anything, Gwen," Pastor Haden said as he and the other men made ready to leave, "you let us know. Anytime of the day or night, you call. We'll be here."

"Thank you." The gratitude in Gwen's face made the moment even more poignant. It wasn't right when any family lost one of its own, but harder still when the woman was left to look after her children, the finances, running a household, and be the backbone all at the same time.

As he headed to the police cruiser, David vowed he wouldn't stop looking until either a body showed up or he died trying.

Harry Senior grabbed his son's shoulder and brought him into a bear hug before David had a chance to get into the police car.

"I'm proud of you, son," Harry Senior said, patting David's back. "For the man you've become and for what you do for a living."

David didn't say anything as his emotions threatened to unravel. Not a good thing for a man in uniform to put on display for anyone to see. But when your father makes a point of letting you know just how proud they are of you, well, any man could be reduced to a child in the matter of a moment.

"Thanks, Dad," David said, trying to sound gruff even as his voice broke. He heard his father chuckle before he was released.

"Why don't you bring yourself to supper?" Harry Senior asked. "It's been a while, and your mother was complaining the other day that she never sees you anymore."

"Yeah, I guess." David rubbed the back of his neck.

"Plus we're going to have a meeting," his father added, stepping towards his second hand sedan. "We're going to see what we can do for Gwen and the boys while Wayne is gone."

David nodded. Knowing his church family they'd not only have Wayne on the prayer list, they'd also surround his family with love and support and anything else they needed to survive the coming days.

Chapter Three

Shivering from the cold, Wayne wrapped his arms around his body to keep warm. He didn't know exactly how long he'd been here, the days were beginning to run together.

He'd been excited about that camping trip with his family. It was nice to see the boys looking forward to it with so much eagerness. They'd reminded him of highly strung puppies.

Gwen even seemed younger, happier, and more carefree. She didn't believe him at first when he'd come home and told her the good news about him giving his life over to Christ. And when his words finally penetrated her doubts, she'd cried against his chest, her tears soaking his shirt, and for the first time he didn't care. He'd pressed her even closer to him, and whispered the kind of things he used to say to her when they were newlyweds.

He hadn't given the mob or the destroyed warehouse any more thought. Just like that old saying; today is the first day of the rest of your life. And as he drove that van into the next town over to do last minute shopping for the trip, he'd felt that it was the first day of the rest of his life with his family.

Wow, he was a lucky man, he'd thought. It'd been years since he'd felt like whistling, but he'd rolled down the windows and whistled as he drove. It wasn't until he was maneuvering the borrowed van along the narrow cliffs that he notices the car behind him.

At first, he tried to convince himself he was being paranoid, but when they inched closer, he got a glimpse of the driver and his pal. The two ugly, stern faces wore sunglasses, but Wayne knew who they were and what they were up to.

They were the mob's angels of death.

Good thing for Wayne he knew the Giver of Life, and he'd never prayed so hard in his life as he did while clutching the wheel with his white-knuckled hands and concentrating on leaving that narrow stretch of cliff road alive.

"If not for my sake, God," he prayed out loud, sweat pouring from his hairline, "but for the sakes of my wife and kids. Not that I've been such a great guy, but they need the man You're making me become. And I need them."

The words were barely out of his mouth when he felt the first nudge from the car behind him. He'd seen enough movies to know what they were up to. They were going to push him off the road into the water below.

To his death.

"Give me strength, God," he cried out. The next hit was harder. The third was the most damaging one. Wayne wrestled with the wheel but it didn't obey. The van went over the cliff, the water rose up to meet him with a greedy welcome.

The impact of the van hitting the water nearly unseated Wayne. The hood crumpled like tinfoil. Thankfully the seatbelt kept him in place. The vehicle immediately began submerging as the strong undercurrent swept it along downstream. Wayne quickly unbuckled and started to move out of the seat when pain shot through his left leg.

He checked it over. Broken.

Not a man given to emotion, Wayne's eyes welled with tears.

How was he going to survive if he had a broken leg? He wondered, blinded by his tears. "It's not for me I'm crying,

God," he said. "I deserve every miserable thing that happens to me. But my family, Gwen, my boys, they'll be devastated when I don't show up with the van."

He might have stayed seated and prayed longer, but given his situation, the sinking van, and his broken leg, Wayne knew he had to struggle or he'd never get out of his predicament alive.

With one last prayer for strength, he gritted his teeth, bundled as much of his supplies into one knapsack and pulled himself out through the side window.

Wayne fell into the swirling water. His gaze fell on rocks up ahead. If he could grab onto them, he might be able to get out of the rushing waves. He didn't stand a chance climbing the sheer face of the cliff without help.

His fingers grabbed the rocks as he passed, caught and then slipped. He battled the raging water, the pain from his leg, and panic at the sound of the roaring falls. It was closer than he'd realized.

There were another larger pile of rocks ahead. They were his last chance before he went over the falls into the rocks below. The falls were synonymous with death; many people had gone over these same cliffs in their vehicles, been swept away by the current and were killed by the rocks below.

Most likely it was the reason why the men chose this stretch of road to push him off. They'd hope the crash killed him, and if that failed, the falls would act as their backup plan.

Blinking against the water slapping into his eyes, Wayne made one last attempt before his strength failed him completely. "God, help me," he cried out as he used the knapsack's strap as a makeshift lasso.

It caught and held.

Wayne pulled himself onto the rocks, but he was still mostly in the water. He hauled air into his lungs and looked around. Despite the grim odds, Wayne refused to give up. But what he needed most was to get out of the water, to dry off, and hope that who ever had pushed him into the river hadn't spotted him surviving.

These cliffs were rumored to have crevices in the rock, Wayne thought. There'd been a documentary not too long ago that he'd watched on television with the boys. With the right circumstances, he just might live to tell the tale.

There'd be a search party looking for him. That thought alone encouraged him.

Gritting his teeth against the pain, Wayne let his gaze travel the side of the rock looking for a break in its surface. It had to be close enough to reach with little effort. The torment of his broken leg was quickly clouding his mind.

"Lord, You know what I need—"

He'd barely begun the prayer when he saw it. A gap. Not five feet from where he clung to the rock. Inching his way to the side, he reached, stretching, his fingers dug into the hard granite and he pulled his way into the opening with a strength he hadn't known he'd had left.

"Thank You, thank You," he repeated, stepping up onto dry ground. It was about four feet deep, carved into the face of the cliff. And it even had a shelf wide enough to accommodate him in a semi-bowed reclining position.

He dropped onto the shelf, and dug through the overstuffed knapsack in search of the first aid kit and supplies. He'd made sure each knapsack had essentials like a first aid kit and something to start a fire with. Years ago, he'd learned to keep things like flashlights and matches in airtight sealed bags where moisture couldn't reach them.

After inhaling two aspirin for the pain, he looked after his broken leg. With two pieces of kindling, he fashioned a makeshift splint.

Chapter Four

David stopped in to see how Gwen and the boys were holding out. It was the eighth day of the search and still no leads. It was as if Wayne had jumped off the end of the world. But he wasn't going to tell Gwen that.

The stress of not knowing where her husband could be was taking its toll on her. If not for the other women rallying around her, Gwen might have given up eating. Even so, despite their help she was starting to look gaunt. But they'd convinced her she needed to keep her strength up if only for the boys.

The boys too were hauling their load of the household burdens. Blake took the car to get groceries after school, and Kev did chores like laundry and mowing the lawn. They also put their regular sibling argue sessions on hold. These weren't the days to squabble over who had the remote to the television in the living room.

"Have you thought of anything else," David asked Gwen as they sat in the living room drinking coffee. "Anything that might give you an idea what could have happened to Wayne?"

She took a long moment to consider that, her brow wrinkled in concentration. "No." She drew out the word. "It's like I've said, the day before he left he told me he had a couple errands to run. He was supposed to be back in about two hours." She glanced up at David as if looking for confirmation for what she remembered. "I can't think of anything else. I'm sorry."

"No, it's me who's sorry for putting you through this," David said, setting aside his half empty coffee mug, and feeling three kinds of a jerk for grilling her during this horrible time. But it was all part of his job, and if they wanted to bring Wayne home it had to be this way.

The telephone rang.

"Kevin, will you please get that?" she asked her youngest son.

The phone stopped in mid-ring. David figured it was most likely someone from the church calling to either check up on Gwen or ask if there was anything she needed.

"Maybe we'd better stop for now," David said, stepping back into officer mode.

"No, please." She held out her hand as if to stop him. "I really am trying. Just give me another few minutes."

His gut told David it was useless. If she hadn't remembered by now then there was very little probability she'd recall something useful about that day. Not without God's help. But if she was willing to try and it made her feel useful, who was he to stop her?

However, before he nodded for her to go ahead, Kev sauntered into the room.

"Who called, dear?" Gwen asked.

"Nothing important." Kev shrugged in that age old way perfected by every teenager. "Just a camera place. Said Dad had ordered a video camera from them, but if he didn't want it to just say so and they'd cancel the order."

"Camera place?" David's mind switched gears. "What was the name of the place?"

"Lens and Something," Kev said, his face blank. "Why?"

"Was it Lens and Film?" David asked holding his breath.

"Yeah." Kev nodded.

"That's twenty miles from here," David said, managing to keep the excitement out of his voice. "Could it be Wayne was headed there to pick up a video camera to take along on the camping trip?"

"That wouldn't surprise me," Gwen said, slowly as if the importance of his question hadn't sunk into her brain yet. "He used to take pictures whenever we went away on vacation."

David almost didn't give her time to fully answer his question. He was out the door and calling for back up on his radio in the cruiser. And then he called the pastor to get the prayer chain going for Wayne again.

Last Sunday Pastor Haden made it clear he didn't want anyone in the congregation entertaining town gossip. "God knows the circumstances," he'd said from the pulpit, making it clear he wasn't going to tolerate hearing any more debatable possibilities behind Wayne's disappearance. Everything from faking his own death, running away with another woman, to alien abduction had made the rounds at the local coffee shop, but the pastor wasn't having his church yield to any such tittle-tattle. They were going to stand united and close rank with a family in need in their congregation, if only to show the town and, essentially, the world that this was the way the Body of Christ looked after its own.

Ten minutes later, David found the tire tracks on the stretch of road leading into the next town. Two other police cars arrived shortly afterwards. This was a well-known dangerous strip of road. It'd be easy enough to go over the edge if a person wasn't familiar with its treacherous twists and turns.

"These aren't fresh," one of the officers said, examining the black tire marks. "And records say the broken rail was reported approximately one week ago."

"I want divers out here," David said in his no-nonsense police tone even as his heart grieved for what they'd discover at the bottom of the river. Chances were slim Wayne could have survived that thirty foot drop into the water. "We need to search the river. See if we can find the van."

The divers showed up within the hour. "That's quite a fall," one of them said as he stood looking over the spot where the tire tracks ended. "But we can't conclude just yet that Wayne didn't survive."

"What are you saying?" David tried not to get his hopes up but his heart sped up in his chest. Please, God, he prayed, if he survived show us where he is.

"I've seen stranger things than this where people lived to tell hair-raising stories." The diver grinned as if looking forward to the challenge of finding a survivor and hearing a new account. Something to tell the boys back at the bar.

David wanted to believe desperately that there was going to be a happy ending to this story yet. But as an officer, he braced himself for the worse possible scenario.

"Okay, suit up," the diver instructed the other four men in his division. "Now remember, we're searching for the van. It might have gone over the falls, but there's always the possibility it snagged on some rocks and sank."

Just before they rappelled themselves down into the water, David heard one of the men say, "Keep an eye out for clefts in the rock. This place is known for them."

David suddenly grinned as the words of one of his favorite hymns played through his head. *He hideth my soul in the cleft of the rock, that shadows a dry thirsty land. He hideth my life in the depths of His love and covers me there with His hand, and covers me there with His hand.*

Tears filled his eyes and he walked a few feet away from the other officers. Somehow, he knew deep in his heart, God had not only preserved Wayne's life, but he'd protected him as well.

The next hour, David waited. His nerves stretched with anticipation but he continued to pray silently.

"Oh great ," one of the officers muttered as a local news reporter arrived. "Just what we need, a circus act. Clowns with cameras. Should be a law against them."

The stress of waiting brought a chuckle from David as he watched the single reporter set up his camera at an angle to get a clear shot of the river not far from where the tire tracks went through the newly fixed railing.

It only took one nosy person to report police activities and the media wasn't long in getting to where the action was going on. However, David knew they were only doing their job, and as long as they didn't interfere, he wouldn't tell them to leave.

"Any sign of Mr. Young yet?" the reporter asked him.

"No."

"What led you here?"

"I have no comments at this time," David said, before he headed for one of the other cruisers where he'd find a thermos of coffee. He hoped the reporter got the hint.

By that evening, the divers found the van but not Wayne. They worked steady until the sun set. A crowd had gathered to watch, and David and the other officers set up a police line.

As the divers stripped out of their wet suits—long after the sun had set—they chattered about the van and the open driver's side window.

"It looks like he got out," one diver said. "No sign of his body though."

David grinned at that and silently thanked God for that hope.

"What say we do this again tomorrow, around first light?" he suggested.

"We'll be here." The divers looked as if they were enjoying themselves. "We haven't been on a call in far too long. We need the practice."

Chapter Five

Wayne's back ached. What he wouldn't give for one hour on the expensive mattress at home. To lie with his arm over Gwen's hip and sleep.

And have a thick barbeque steak for supper. To listen to the boys argue. To hear the crickets in the back yard as the sun set behind the mountains. To take a bath. To put on clean clothes.

Hey, if he was going to dream, he might as well make it a good one, Wayne decided as he rolled over onto his stomach to give his back a rest. However, even that was uncomfortable.

The first few days, he thought he'd die of boredom. Not much challenge in a cave wall with nothing to do but listen to the water roaring downstream. He recited Bible verses that he'd thought were long forgotten from when he'd attended Sunday school as a kid.

And he sang hymns, and prayed, and thought about how God had blessed him all through his life. That'd he'd married Gwen in itself was a miracle, but then the boys had come along and he'd never been happier.

How he missed their beautiful faces.

He choked on his tears, and prayed for them to be strong through this ordeal until he was either rescued…or his body found.

Would anyone find him? He'd asked the Lord that question what felt like a million years ago. The answer that came to him might not have helped him a month ago, but now it seemed perfect.

Where can I flee for your presence, if I go up to the heavens you are there, if I make my bed in the depths you are there.

It was the verse Pastor Haden quoted the day Wayne went to talk to him and confess his thoughts of suicide.

More tears rushed into his eyes, and Wayne lowered his head. It wasn't a reaction to self-pity, rather he couldn't believe how blessed he was that God truly was with him, in this little cave, miles away from family and friends who most likely were mourning him.

They might even have had a memorial service.

Wayne suddenly laughed as he pictured a scene out of Tom Sawyer, but instead of Tom and Huckleberry Finn interrupting their own funeral it was Wayne surprising everyone. It warmed him to imagine how his wife and sons would react. They'd run and wrap their arms around him, welcoming him home with tears and joy.

"Please, God," he breathed the prayer, "make that a reality. Let me go home, to my family. I don't care what happens after that. I'll sell everything I have and go into the ministry, if that's what You want me to do. I'm putty in Your hands."

"Hey buddy, are you waiting for a cab?"

Wayne jumped when the grinning man in the diving suit leaned into the opening of the crevice.

Wayne's mind went blank at the shock of seeing another human being.

"I hope I didn't catch you at a bad time," the diver quipped when he failed to receive a reply.

"Praise God," were the first words out of Wayne's mouth. "I'm going home."

"How did you find me?" Wayne asked the men standing around him by the side of the road an hour later. He huddled under a blanket someone had wrapped around his shoulders as an EMT examined his badly mending broken leg.

"God showed us the way," David answered before anyone else took the credit. "Without His help, you probably would have died out there."

"I know." Wayne closed his eyes in gratitude. Exhausted from the ordeal, he wanted to sleep, but needed to ask, "Where's Gwen and the boys?"

"They're going to meet you at the hospital," David said. "They already heard the good news."

The ambulance driver and the other EMT helped Wayne get settled on the stretcher, hooked him up to an I.V. drip and then carefully hoisted him into the back of the open doors of the ambulance.

"Do I need to tell you what happened?" Wayne asked as David stood next to the opened doors. "About the guys who blew out my tire?"

"We'll worry about that after the doctors have had a chance to set that leg," Officer David said. "And after your wife and kids can smother you with affection."

"Yeah," Wayne let his head fall back on the stretcher, "that sounds Heavenly to me."

That following Sunday, Wayne escorted his clinging wife and grinning sons to church. As they walked—he stumped along on his cast—down the aisle together, the congregation rose as one giving the family a standing ovation.

Through the entire ordeal, not only had Wayne's life been spared, but he'd also made a decision to follow Christ.

Pastor Haden stepped down from the pulpit and met them half way in the aisle with outstretched arms. He hugged them, as if blessing them as a family. Others in the congregation moved forward to embrace them as well, and when they couldn't get close enough to touch Wayne, Gwen or the boys, they hugged each other.

David stood back and watched, overwhelmed by the scene and flooded with the sense of privilege, that God had used him to help find a lost brother.

When the congregation finally returned to their seats, and Gwen and the boys sat down, the pastor beckoned for Wayne to come forward and give his testimony.

"You have no idea," Wayne addressed the congregation, as tears ran unchecked down his face. "What it means to me to stand here looking at your faces. A month ago, standing here and witnessing for the Lord wouldn't have been on my agenda. I was actually contemplating suicide."

He shifted his weight from the cast to his other foot when his voice broke. "I came here one Monday afternoon to see the pastor. He was supposed to tell me that God would okay my decision to end my life, to get my family out of harm's way." He struggled to maintain his dignity, as tears of gratitude gushed down his face. "There were some very dangerous men who saw me as a threat and they needed to get me out of their way.

"But the pastor quickly put me to rights about suicide." Mopping his tears with a handful of tissue, he sent Pastor Haden a smile filled with thanks. "And while I was stuck in that cave, I had a lot of time to think about my life, and to get in some fellowship time with God. Now I know how Jonah felt, but he'd only had a three day stint."

A few tear-filled chuckles raced around the sanctuary.

"Since returning home, I found out my wife has been praying for me to get saved for years." He sent Gwen a covert wink. "Not that she'd want me to go over a cliff in a borrowed van to get to that level of dependence on God." He paused. "I hope."

More laughter; stronger this time.

"I've also learned that while my reputation was being shredded by the community, on account of my disappearance, this church," he sent another meaningful glance around him at the faces he'd soon put names to, "my new family, stood up for me, prayed for me, loved my wife and kids unconditionally, and made it clear that until the facts came out no one was going to jump to conclusions. I thank you for that. I may not know you yet, but I love you. My only regret is I didn't know the depths of your kindness and love until it was nearly too late. God bless you all."

Wayne headed for his place beside his wife while the church thundered with applause, and shouts of thanksgiving.

"That's beautiful," Jane whispered, wiping her own damp eyes with a tissue. "If church had been like that when I was growing up there's no way I would have walked away."

"Amen," Mike agreed.

"But what about the mob?" Jane asked as if suddenly remembering how Wayne ended up in the cave in the first place. "Weren't they waiting for him when he was found?"

"Nope." Mike grinned. "I don't know how God worked it out, it's a police hush-hush matter, even Officer David won't say anything, but there haven't been any repercussions. The ones who'd bombed the warehouse were charged and sent to prison. And Wayne got out of his business, has taken his love for film and started a company that specializes in making Christian movies."

"I wonder if I've heard of any of his productions."

Faith named a couple.

"Those were his? They were good," Jane said, her eyes round with astonishment. "I have to meet him."

"Come to church this Sunday," Faith said, eager to press the point home, "and you will. He and Gwen and the boys never miss a service."

"I just might." Jane nodded as the three settled into the living room with fresh mugs of coffee.

"You must be tired of listening to us ramble on," Faith said.

"Are you kidding me?" Jane laughed. "I'm like a little kid needing a candy fix. What else you got?"

Faith looked over at Mike, her eyes filled with mischief. "What do you think, Mike? Think she'd like hearing about the blues?"

"Oh yeah." Mike nodded. "She'll love that one for sure."

The Blues Brothers

Prologue

The church was looking for musical talent, and Pastor Haden asked Sam, the church's choir leader, to take over the ministry. The man who normally oversaw Sunday service singing specials was being transferred with his job, and it left a gaping hole in the church program.

"You know what we're looking for," the pastor said as Sam sat at the piano in the sanctuary on Tuesday afternoon and played a few notes.

"I have an inkling." Sam didn't take his gaze from the piano. This was his private time to worship the Lord while he planned what the choir would sing the following Sunday. "Leave it between me and Jesus."

"Thank you," Pastor Haden said before he walked down the aisle towards his office.

Sam continued to play, pray, and concentrate on what the Lord would say to him that day. However, the moment the pastor had approached him on the subject, two faces came to Sam's mind. Leroy and Charlie.

He'd seen them a few months ago at the mall, they'd stopped and chatted with him. Sam didn't believe in coincidences. Perhaps God had something in store for those two that even they didn't realize.

Sam remembered their conversation, both of them had said the same thing; that they were too caught up in the secular music scene and didn't think God would ever want them to play music in church. Boy, were they wrong.

Chapter One

[Leroy]

The sun beat down on Leroy's bare head while he sat on the front step of his family home and experimented with the second hand guitar he'd picked up at a yard sale a couple weeks earlier. He'd always known he had natural talent, he could play any piece by ear. Mama always made a big deal over his ability, and bragged him up in front of friends and family.

That's when they'd challenge him to prove it, and he'd get out the guitar, strum a few bars and sing. He normally played hymns, blues style. Every person asked basically the same question, why wasn't he playing professionally?

Their praise alone was worth the calluses he'd built up on the ends of his fingers. For years, he'd wanted to bring his music to church, but the opportunity never presented itself. For one thing, his church didn't want anything other than an organ in their midst during services. And for another, the minister didn't much care for any kind of music other than slow, sanctimonious pieces. Even some of the songs in the hymnals were snubbed because they were too upbeat.

Leroy closed his eyes and shook his head while the music continued to flow from his fingers over the guitar strings. Every day he wondered how he'd ever managed to hear a salvation message at that church, the kind that brought him to his knees in prayer and confession. But he had; he'd given his life to God not six months ago, and the more he fell in love with his Savior and the Bible the more annoyed he grew with the minister at his church.

No wonder people got a bad feeling towards God, Leroy thought as he played Amazing Grace. As long as there were self-righteous people sitting in pews and feeling like good people because they gave their money and attended church regularly then the battle would continue to be won by the enemy.

And every day people died and souls went to Hell.

Leroy's heart clenched at the thought, and he stopped playing the song. The guitar went back into its case as Leroy decided he needed to take a walk down to what the people in his neighborhood called 'the corner'.

The corner was actually the town square, with a small park in the centre. Benches were set up for people to sit and relax, to watch the water fountain, surrounded by nature. Various businesses ran parallel to the street, a bookstore, shoe store, and barber. It was where people met and talked and enjoyed the day together.

A day like today, Leroy thought as he made his way downtown. Maybe, when he had enough pieces, he could play his music in the park. Until then, he'd just have to be content with honing his skill on his front step.

Or did he?

The question popped into his head when he passed one of the houses on his way to the park. Up on the open porch sat a group of men with various instruments, jamming.

Playing blues no less.

Enthralled, Leroy stood on the sidewalk and listened. The music was good, professional, but not Christian. However, he didn't let that stop him from enjoying their talent. Their playing spoke of years of experience. The way the oldest man handled the guitar made Leroy wish he had half his talent. Another man had a harmonica, and another sat behind a portable electric keyboard.

They were good.

A small crowd gathered to listen and enjoy the impromptu concert. Children played within ear shot of the music while their parents snapped their fingers or danced. No one seemed in a hurry to leave.

It was Leroy's first taste of what club life offered. Not that he was interested in that side of the music business, but he longed to play along with these guys. However, he was too shy to ask.

All that week, the weather held, and Leroy found himself drawn downtown, or more to the point, to the house where the men had jammed on the porch. Sure enough, they were there again, and so was the crowd.

However, two days later it rained. Leroy was disappointed. He'd been looking forward to hearing more tunes. Every evening he'd practice the music he'd heard the group play, able to play any piece by ear. It didn't take long for him to figure out the notes.

Not one to be discouraged, Leroy headed to the corner that afternoon despite the downpour. The crowd was noticeably absent, and so were the musicians except for one; the oldest man who played guitar.

"You don't mind if I listen, do you, sir?" Leroy asked when the man glanced over at him.

"Help yourself," the man said in a kind voice. His grin showed off a missing front tooth.

Leroy sat on the porch floor and watched and listened. Now that it was just the one man playing, he realized where the true talent of the group lay. The others were good, but they had nothing on the guitar player.

Up close, Leroy got to see the man's fingers zip up and down the neck of the guitar, blurring as he played.

"What's your name, boy?" the man asked when he took a break long enough to reach for the glass of ice tea beside him on the end table.

"Leroy." He didn't know why it felt like he'd been given a great honor when the man asked him the simple question, but he did.

"You can call me Fingers." He grinned again, patting the guitar with his free hand. "On account of the way I play this lady."

"Sir, Mr. Fingers, you are the best thing I've ever heard," Leroy said, his words filled with awe. It didn't matter he was nearly eighteen, the man made him feel like a kid meeting a rock star.

"You sound like you know a thing or two about music," Fingers said, wiping his mouth on the back of his sleeve.

"Well," Leroy rubbed the back of his neck, "I pick at my guitar."

"Let's hear what you can do." Fingers held out his expensive flat-top.

Leroy couldn't believe the older man was willing to hand over his guitar to a stranger.

Wiping his suddenly damp palms down the sides of his pants, Leroy stood up and then reached for the guitar. He settled on the wicker sofa and proceeded, with slightly shaking hands, to play the first piece he'd heard Fingers' group practice together, the one he'd spent hours trying to figure out.

"Not bad," Fingers complimented him when Leroy strummed the last note. "Not bad at all. You got raw talent, boy."

"Thank you, sir." The fact that the comment came from a professional was the greatest validation Leroy received in his life.

"You should look into taking lessons."

"Would you teach me?" Leroy asked. "Sir?" he added out of respect.

"Well, I don't know…"

"I can pay."

"Don't need your money." Fingers hooked the strap around his neck and began strumming the guitar again.

"Please, sir. There's no one I could get to teach me, not like you." Leroy would beg if he had to.

Fingers didn't speak for a few minutes, and Leroy hardly breathed, not sure if the older man had dismissed him from his mind or was considering his request. He really hoped it was the latter.

"Okay," Fingers finally said. "I'll give you a month. If I see improvement, you can play along with the band. If not, well, we'll see."

"Thank you, sir." Leroy nearly whooped with joy, but managed to maintain a dignified façade. "You won't regret this. I got talent.

Chapter Two

[Charlie]

"Where do you think you're going, young man?"

"Out." Charlie paused at the front door, jacket in hand. It was enough to hear the anger in his father's voice; he didn't need to see it in his face as well.

"Don't you have piano practice?"

"I deserve a break," Charlie said from between his gritted teeth.

"Oh? Have you been offered the opportunity to play piano at our church?"

"No." Charlie hated it when his father was sarcastic. It made him feel like a five year old instead of seventeen.

"What was that?" His father asked, while Charlie knew he'd heard his answer.

"I said no, sir."

"Then I suggest you put your jacket in the closet, and get back to the living room and practice for the next two hours."

"But—"

"Do what I say, Charlie."

Heaving a sigh, Charlie obeyed, muttering beneath his breath at the injustice of living under his father's iron fist. What he wouldn't give for his father to wake up and realize he didn't want to play piano: not now, not ever.

If Charlie had his way, he'd buy a set of drums and pound out his daily frustration and anger. Loud enough to bring the cops to their door a dozen times a day. But he didn't see that happening any time soon. His father was more determined to see him formally educated in as many musical instruments as possible—with the exception of drums.

Beginning at the age of five, Charlie was forced to endure endless hours at the piano, clarinet, trombone, classical guitar, and cello. However, he'd thrown a temper tantrum when his father considered adding the harp to the list. No way was he going to play a sissy harp.

The only way he'd ever admit he didn't mind learning to play those instruments would be if someone pulled his toenails out with tweezers. Music lessons had always been a sore spot between him and his father.

Sitting down at the piano, Charlie scowled. He didn't feel like playing Beethoven, Chopin, or Mozart. In a fit of rebellion, he cranked up the volume on his electric piano and let loose his own version of an Elvis Presley tune.

The sound of his father thumping down the stairs brought a satisfied grin to Charlie's face.

"What are you doing?" His father roared out the question. "Stop that devil's music right now."

"Is that what it was?" Charlie feigned innocence if only to see the vein in his father's forehead throb. Sadly enough, it'd be the highlight of his day. "I was only doing what you told me to; practice."

"That isn't what I meant," his father said through his clenched teeth. "Stick to the hymns. And that's it. One more outburst like that and you'll be grounded for a month. I'll personally have you chained to that piano."

"Ja. Ja." To soothe ruffled feathers, Charlie settled on a more sedate hymn from the eighteenth century, earning him his father's instant approval.

"Good. Now, can I trust you'll behave?"

Charlie nodded without pausing. When the door closed behind his father's departing back, Charlie sighed.

What he wouldn't give to be a normal teenager; dating, hanging out with his buddies at the mall, and driving around in a car. If he was allowed to have an afterschool job, he'd buy one. But here he was, stuck to the piano as if he really was chained to it.

After five minutes of grumbling to himself, he gave his full attention to the next hymn that seemed to jump from his fingers to the keys.

I Surrender All.

His shoulders slumped in his own personal submission, not to his father, but to God. Charlie had bowed his knees at the altar when he'd been a child, two years after his mother passed away.

Things hadn't been easy for his dad. Taking care of a kid, working full time to keep a roof over their head, trying to be both parents. To outsiders, it might look like his father was ruling him without mercy, but he knew better. A lot of sacrifices were made so Charlie could have lessons. His father wanted more for his son than he'd had. It would have made him so proud if Charlie played piano at the church, but it wasn't something Charlie was interested in. He wanted a normal life.

After two hours, Charlie quit practicing. A glance at his watch said it was still early enough to meet with his buddies. This time, he'd only go with his father's approval, if only to keep the peace.

"That was two hours?" Charlie's father looked up from where he sprawled on his bed, reading the newspaper.

"Yes."

"Ok. It's Friday night. You can stay out until midnight."

"Thanks, Dad." Charlie grinned. Sometimes his dad could show leniency, and he almost felt guilty for where he was going. Almost.

"But I don't want you near that boy's place, the one with the drums."

And then he could be the domineering parent again, Charlie thought as resentment slithered into his heart. How could he possibly know what he'd been planning?

"I'll be home at twelve," Charlie said, purposely not agreeing not to go to Kyle's house.

"We'll do another set," Kyle said, adjusting the volume on his bass. "Then we'll call it a night."

"Ok." Charlie hid his grin. Kyle was under the delusion they were playing for a live audience instead of practicing in his dad's garage.

"What's all that noise out here?" Kyle's father demanded. "I can't hear the game."

"C'mon, Dad, we're working here," Kyle said, whining. Charlie knew exactly what his father would say if he tried that on him.

You're not a child, Charlie. You're old enough to have a driver's license. Or would you prefer I get a booster seat for you?

"You're kidding," Kyle's dad said. "I thought you were playing my old records."

"Nah." Kyle's chest swelled at the remark.

"And you were playing drums?" The older man turned the question on Charlie.

"Ye-eah." Charlie hoped that information wouldn't get back to his father.

"You're good." Kyle's dad entered the garage and crossed his arms over his chest. "I mean, you're really good."

"Take that as high praise, man," Kyle said to Charlie. "I don't even get that from him."

"That's because you stink," his father said, but his smile took the edge off his insult. "How long you been playing, Charlie?"

"What time is it?" Charlie joked.

"No, I mean lessons."

"I showed him the ropes a couple weeks ago," Kyle said. "He picked up most of the stuff on his own."

"You really are a boy wonder when it comes to music," the older man said, awed by Charlie's skill. "Listen, anytime you want to play here, feel free. I used to play drums in a band years ago. If you have any questions, the doors open."

"Thanks." Charlie's face warmed up at the compliment, and wished his father was nearly as supportive when it came to the drums. Their relationship might have improved dramatically.

Chapter Three

[Leroy]

Apparently there was more to life than talent, Leroy thought cynically as he leaned against the bar clutching his watered down whisky. For the past ten years he'd been playing smoky night clubs, popping pills, and basically existing in a world that had lost its shine.

When he'd proved his worth to Fingers and joined the band, church and God somehow got pushed to the backburner as they toured the countryside. His desire to serve the Lord might have tampered down, but hadn't gone away completely.

What he wouldn't give to leave these dives and go play blues-style gospel music in church. Or any place for God, he amended pushing his drink aside and letting his face fall onto the cold surface of the bar.

"Come on, Leroy," Chris, one of the guys from his group, poked him in the shoulder. "One more set, then you can get a girl from the crowd and go back to your hotel room."

When Leroy merely groaned at that, Chris shouldered Leroy's arm and led him back to the stage where their instruments were set up. "Just a couple more songs, old man," he cajoled.

It would have been just the thing Leroy needed to hear to rev up his motivation, but for the past months the ache in the pit of his stomach told him something was passing him by. Last night he'd found the Bible in his motel room's night stand and he'd opened it to one of his favorite passages. The story of the loaves and fishes.

That's what Leroy wanted. For Jesus to bless his music and to feed the souls of God's people through it. But no one in their right mind would even consider Leroy for that kind of ministry. They'd take one look at the life he'd led and pass him off as a lost cause. Not that he'd blame them.

Leroy picked up his guitar and strummed a couple notes as the other guys made their way back up on stage. For the next hour, they played favorites from their latest c.d. and then quit for the night.

They left as the roadies began loading up the black trailer parked in the alley with sound equipment and instruments. Normally, Leroy didn't let anyone touch his guitar but tonight he didn't have it in him to care.

The other guys lingered around the bar drinking—which didn't make sense because their motel rooms had bottles of liquor waiting for them—before heading out. Leroy ignored their invitations to join them, opting instead to head out the door and take a walk. He'd noticed the lay of the town when they drove in that afternoon. One street reminded him of the 'corner' back in his home town, and he figured it'd be nice to take a walk and pretend he was home again, watching Fingers play on the front porch.

It was after two am and the street was deserted. The air was warm and humid; refreshing after an evening spent at a bar. He wanted only a few moments alone to think about his future. Did he have one? Probably not, if he didn't give up the booze and drugs.

He sat down on one of the benches in the park, leaned his head back and stared up at the starry sky. "God," he started to pray, "I know I've done some bad things. Fact is, I've made the biggest mistake of my life turning my back on You and my roots. I know

if my parents saw me right now they'd be ashamed. I've taken the gift You gave me and polluted it. Things are so bad I don't even enjoy playing music anymore. But I know You give second chances. Could You give me one? Could You get me out of this life?"

Leroy didn't know he'd spent the night on that park bench until the morning sun burned his eyelids. He rubbed the back of his throbbing neck.

Checking his watch, it shocked him that it was after seven am. He'd never done anything like this before, sleeping out on a park bench. And yet it seemed fitting, another dose of reality that if he didn't get away from the drugs and booze this was the future waiting for him.

Apparently, he even looked the part when an early morning walker passed by and questioned him.

"How long has it been since you had a hot meal, young man?" the stranger asked, kindness etched in his concerned eyes.

Leroy shrugged. He really didn't remember. Most days started with a bottle.

"I know where you can clean up and get something to eat and it won't cost you a thing."

Any other time Leroy would have been offended, but today he tossed his pride aside. "It's been a while since I've been clean," he said, but he wasn't talking about a shower. He meant the kind of cleansing he'd find at the foot of the cross where his Savior had died.

"My church offers a breakfast program to those who are hungry." The man pointed with his thumb to the end of the street, not fifty feet from where Leroy had passed out on the park bench. "There, you'll be able to shower, eat, and talk to someone. I'm on my way there if you'd like to tag along."

That was the best offer Leroy'd had in years. And he wasn't about to turn it down. "Thanks, man. I'd appreciate it." He got to his feet, albeit a little unsteadily considering the position he'd slept in and the amount of liquor he'd consumed during his gig.

"My name's Sam," the man introduced himself, holding out his hand in warm welcome. "I'm the music director at the church."

"No kidding. Huh!" Leroy chuckled, realizing exactly how God had answered his prayers.

"What's so funny?" Sam asked not sounding the least bit offended, just interested in sharing the joke.

"You could say I'm into music."

"What kind?"

"Blues." Leroy didn't want to admit the reason why he was in town in the first place but now wasn't the time to hide the truth. "My boys and I played at the bar last night."

"Oh." Understanding dawned in Sam's eyes. "I hope you weren't insulted when I offered you a meal and shower."

"Nope." Leroy shook his head, mindful of the headache jabbing at his temples. "In fact, you gave me a privilege that hasn't come my way in years. Not many churches open their arms to a blues player with drug and alcohol issues like mine."

"Brother, God welcomes all the wounded, the lost, and hurting into His fold."

It was exactly what Leroy needed to hear.

They made small talk as they entered the church. Sam introduced Leroy to Pastor Haden who in turn made Leroy feel like he'd just come home. Nothing about the larger man remotely reminded Leroy of the Spirit-quenching pastor from his first church.

Comfortable with the other two men, he confessed his drug and alcohol issues, his walking away from God, and they listened without judging him. Instead, they fed him, handed him a towel and a bar of soap, directed him to the shower, and handed him an almost brand new pair of jeans and shirt in his size.

Afterwards, Sam took Leroy aside and they talked for hours. Leroy told his newfound friend the story of how he'd gotten involved in blues music in the first place, learning to play guitar, and how it had eventually led him down the road to the seedy side of life.

"But I don't want it anymore," Leroy said. "I want to go back to God, to surrender every part of me, even if it means laying aside my music."

"God gave you that talent, Leroy," Sam said. "He wouldn't want you to sacrifice it, but He would want you to play music that honors Him."

"Yes." Leroy's face lit up with the knowledge that he wouldn't have to give up the guitar.

"Why don't we pray?" Sam asked. "I'll start."

Leroy nodded, closing his eyes. He desperately wanted to repent of his rebellion, and all the things that came between him and the Lord for years. After getting his heart right with his Lord again, Leroy truly felt he'd found a church he'd like to attend.

That Sunday, Leroy stood in front of the congregation, gave his testimony and played the blues-style worship song God had given him the hour Leroy had repented of his sins. He'd never have thought it possible that he'd be welcomed back to church, but the congregation acted as if he'd been a member for years, and loved him like family.

He was home.

Chapter Four

[Charlie]

"I think we should drop this song from our set."

Charlie looked up from the drums when one of the band members chose that moment during practice to air his grievances.

"What's wrong with it?" the lead singer asked, grabbing hold of the mic and pinning the guitar player with a gimlet glare.

Charlie put his head back down behind the drums. This was warming up to be one of the group's infamous arguments. And he was sick of it.

They'd lost countless chances to play live because of their reputation for getting into fights and cancelling at the last minute. As far as Charlie was concerned, the band was going no where fast.

"It's stupid," the guitar player said without qualifying the question with a good reason.

"You mean you can't get the rhythm." The lead singer snorted with derision.

"Well, if that's how you feel," the guitar player yanked the strap off from around his neck, and headed for his guitar case, "I quit."

"No you don't." Charlie contradicted him. Every eye in the room turned in his direction, mostly out of surprise because Charlie never got involved in any of their disagreements. "Because I quit."

A collective gasp went up around him.

"You're not serious," the guitar player said, his mouth dropping open.

"I guess I am," Charlie said, setting his stool back so he could tear down his drums. He'd paid a lot of money for that set and he wasn't going to walk out of there without them. Knowing them, they'd sell them to buy another low-grade sound system.

"Charlie, this is crazy," the lead singer said. "What are we going to do without you?"

"Guess you're gonna find out." He shrugged. It took him twenty minutes to take the set apart and carefully load it into his car. And every one of those minutes the guys tried to convince him to stay. However, he wasn't budging on his decision this time.

"But we have a gig this Saturday night," the lead singer said

"What were you going to do without a guitar player when he quit?" Charlie hauled the last of the drums out of the garage. "Improvise or just cancel like you normally do?"

"Is that what this is about?" the guitar player asked. "You know we're always joking around. It's what we do."

"No, what you do is fight, break up and ruin our reputation as a band," Charlie said. "I'm tired of it." He took one last look at the distressed faces of his former group.

"Far as I can tell, I've made the most sacrifices to be in this band. You're all acting like high school kids with more ego than talent. I want to deal with professionals. See you around."

Charlie hadn't been kidding when he mentioned personal sacrifices. He couldn't begin to count the number of times he'd had to lie to his dad about where he was going, the close calls he'd had when his father mentioned showing up for one of his concerts.

His father thought he was playing piano or the cello, when in fact he'd been playing drums for a rock band. Charlie grimaced at what might have happened if his dad had walked in on one of those performances.

As it was, he'd managed to outmaneuver his father every time; using any excuse including cancellations. However, to completely cover his tracks, he'd played piano the odd time whenever someone was needed to cover the regular piano player at church. That had satisfied his father, but it'd made Charlie feel like the biggest hypocrite on the planet.

His passion for God had cooled off over the years, more so when he played with the band. But he couldn't help it, he wasn't happy playing piano.

And Charlie was tired of being someone other than himself.

So, when he was old enough, he got a day job selling pianos—ironically enough—and covertly tried to make a go of weekend gigs with the band under the guise of music conventions with his job.

The thought of being without his band didn't scare Charlie. He'd already checked the classifieds in the newspaper and found a few groups hosting try outs. The most professional one that he'd heard of was in fact a heavy metal group. It wasn't necessarily his style of music but he was willing to try anything if it meant becoming a successful drum player.

His interview was at seven that night. With two hours to kill, Charlie stopped to have supper at a restaurant. He didn't want to go home and be unnerved by his father. Chances were good it'd be just the time his father would demand he practice piano. The very thought of playing classical tunes sent chills down Charlie's spine.

At seven o'clock, Charlie stepped into the auditorium. The group looked exactly as he'd expected them to; long free flowing hair, black eyeliner, and torn jeans. They were mostly men, with one female vocal.

"Hey, look at the nerd," one of the guys shouted out, snickering when Charlie entered the building.

Charlie didn't mind the insult. He knew what he looked like, the façade to keep his father from catching on to his after hour habits. His short hair, his university professor clothes: pressed dress slacks and pin stripe shirt layered with a tan colored sweater.

"We don't play Buddy Holly stuff," the woman at the mic said, joining in on the fun at Charlie's expense.

"That's good," Charlie said, grinning confidently. "Because I don't play Buddy Holly stuff."

"Show us what you got then," the lead guitarist invited, pointing to the drums behind him.

Charlie jumped up on the stage, feeling the adrenalin pump through his veins as it always did when he got a set of drum sticks in his hands. That and knowing he was about to blow their minds and expectations with his drum solo.

He'd barely begun when the band members joined him in an impromptu jam session. Within moments, Charlie forgot he was auditioning he was so caught up in the thrill of drumming and feeling a part of something big.

"That was good," the female vocal said, her sneer long gone.

"You got talent kid," the guitar player agreed. "We'll get back to you on it."

"Sure."

"Oh, who are we kidding," the lead guitarist said, chuckling. "You're the best audition we've ever had, even better than our last drummer. We'll hire you, on one condition."

Charlie cringed. He knew what was coming. It was inevitable to keep up with the image of a heavy metal group.

"You can keep the short hair," the guitarist said, "but you got to change your clothes."

"Not a problem," Charlie said, shrugging, vastly relieved. The clothes he could hide from his father.

"We'll go shopping," the woman said, looking every bit pleased at the prospect of going to the mall.

"Congratulations then," the group said, then proceeded with introductions and a schedule of their practice times and upcoming concerts. "Think you can handle all that?" Spike, the lead guitarist asked.

"As long as there's a drum involved," Charlie said, "You can depend on me."

"I like him," Tiffany said, smiling broadly. "He's got class."

Chapter Five

"Hey, Charlie," Carl, the band's manager, shouted above the voices in the bar. "I got a message for you."

Charlie looked up from where he talked with Tiffany. Since going on tour together, they started seeing each other. Like the drums, she was everything his father would disapprove of. Her clothes, her hair, makeup-things that screamed a sinful lifestyle and Charlie liked her even more for that.

"What is it?" Charlie took a drink of his beer and waited for Carl to continue.

"Your dad. He's had a stroke."

"What?" Charlie nearly choked. He slammed his beer down on the bar. "Where is he?"

Carl gave the name of the hospital that had admitted him.

"I got to go see him."

"You can't leave now," Tiffany said, her upper lip lifting in a sneer as she grabbed onto his arm. "Especially for your old man. Let him die. You got more important things, like performing with the group."

Suddenly, Charlie saw Tiffany in a new light. Sure, she was beautiful but not as much as he'd originally thought. Her lack of compassion tainted his feelings for her.

"I have to," he said, trying to loosen her grip on him. "No matter what anyone else thinks, he's still my father."

"If you ditch us now, you won't be welcomed back," she snarled even as he turned and hurried away. "And don't think I'll give you another chance."

Charlie didn't care. As much as he'd rebelled over the years, his father was the one mainstay of his life. Sure they fought like proverbial cats and dogs, but they loved each other.

At the hospital, Charlie found out what room his father was in, and his condition.

"I'm here, Dad," he said, taking the seat next to his father's bed. Exhaustion followed hard on his heels after a sleepless night trying to book a flight back home.

Charlie looked down at his father's sleeping form. As his gaze took in the I.V., and the heart monitor, guilt tightened the knots in his stomach. He remembered all the arguments he'd had with this man over the years, how big and intimidating he'd seemed. Now he looked like a shriveled up shadow of his former self.

Charlie bowed his head, and let the tears flow. He'd give up all his talent if it meant he could save his father's life.

"Hi." A nurse came in to the room and bee-lined for the patient.

"Is he going to make it?" Charlie asked in a hushed tone.

"Are you his son?" She didn't look up as she changed the I.V. fluid bag.

"Yes. I only just got here." He clenched his hands together; the knuckles turned white. "I know he's had a stroke. But he'll live, right?"

"It's too early to know fully the extent of the damage," she said. "Usually, the patients have paralyses, and he'll probably need therapy."

"But he'll survive?" Charlie persisted.

"Most likely." She nodded. "The doctor will be here in the morning. He can give you more answers."

"Thank you." Charlie's head dropped forward again as she left the room. "This is my fault, Dad. I never should have rebelled against you. But things are going to change, I promise."

The doctor's prognosis, hours later, was less comforting than the nurse's.

"Your father is paralyzed on his left side," he told Charlie without so much as blinking an eye in sympathy. "He'll need physio to help him regain some of his strength, but chances are he'll need to go into a special care home."

Devastated by that information, Charlie didn't leave his father's side until the nurses chased him away to get some sleep. "There's no sense in getting sick yourself," one young woman told him. "Go home, clean up, eat, and rest. You'll be more help to your father in a better state of mind."

"Ok."

Charlie did manage to do as ordered, but the guilt hung on. Tears clogged his throat and he knew he couldn't go back and weep all over his father. His dad didn't like tears. They were a sign of weakness, especially in a man.

But Charlie knew where he could go and let out his emotions: church. He didn't want to go to the one where his father attended; they'd given up on him a long time ago when he stopped attending their services. However, he'd heard stories about the one downtown; how they opened their doors to people whom society turned their back on.

The church doors were unlocked when Charlie tried them. Somewhere inside the building someone was playing the piano reverently. Normally, Charlie would turn his nose up at that kind of music, but not tonight. If someone could help ease the torment in his heart, he'd never scorn the piano again.

"Can I help you?" A large man asked. The depths of compassion in the larger man's eyes evoked the emotions Charlie desperately wanted to release.

"C…can I talk to someone?"

"Anyone in particular?" the man asked.

"No."

"I'm the pastor here," he introduced himself. "Pastor Haden. I've got all the time you need, if you want to talk to me."

Charlie nodded wordlessly. He followed Pastor Haden down the hall into a small office. They sat down opposite each other, but Charlie didn't know where to begin.

"Take your time," the pastor said, "I'll read some Scripture until you're ready." He flipped a few pages in his black Bible and stated he'd be reading from the book of John.

Charlie soaked up the words the pastor read out loud. It didn't seem like any time had passed until he glanced at his watch and realized it was nearly eight thirty. He needed to get back to the hospital, but first he had to talk.

"I'm Charlie," he began, "I used to be a Christian, but I turned my back on God a long time ago. And now I want to make it right."

Pastor Haden listened in silence as Charlie lanced the sorrow and pain he'd carried around with him for a lifetime, until he came to the part about his father being in the hospital and why.

"Your father would never blame you for his stroke," the pastor said, "from what I can surmise from your story. He sacrificed a lot for you to have the things he thought were best for you."

"Yeah." Charlie closed his eyes as guilt sliced through him again.

"And I know Someone else who made a sacrifice for you to give you life and give it more abundantly."

"Isn't it too late for me?" Charlie asked, hoping he still had a chance. "I mean, I rebelled against God."

"A lot of us do that," Pastor Haden said. "But rebellion isn't the unpardonable sin. If you're truly sorry, and confess your sins to God, and give over total control of your life to Him, He will always welcome you home. I'm going to pray. You can join in at any time."

The pastor led him in a prayer, confessing his sinful state, and asking for God's forgiveness through the power of the blood that His only begotten Son had shed on Calvary. Afterwards, Charlie felt the burden of guilt roll off his shoulders.

Epilogue

[Two Weeks Ago]

"You really put your heart into practice tonight, Charlie," Sam said when Charlie let the last note of the piano fade away.

"Yeah," Charlie grinned. "My dad's going to be here on Sunday."

Sam didn't need anyone to tell him just how proud Charlie's father was of his boy. Charlie himself had told Sam about his testimony and that after he gave his life to God he'd confessed his lies to his dad and they were working things out between them. Charlie had even brought his father back home, once he had recovered enough from the stroke, and had hired full-time care givers.

Sam couldn't help grinning at the newest two members of his blues band. Leroy manipulated sounds out his guitar that could make any seasoned blues player cry with envy, but Charlie tickled the ivories like someone born to play.

He couldn't believe how good God was to bring these two men to his church from a wild life of night clubs, drinking, and drugs.

"That's cool, man," Leroy said, setting aside his guitar. "I invited an old friend of mine to hear us play too."

"Fingers?" Sam guessed.

"You got it." Leroy winked. "He's wanted to hear us play for a while."

"And he's in for a real treat," Sam said.

"Yep, and our music will sound okay too." Leroy laughed.

"God is good," Charlie said sincerely. "God is so good."

Sam and Leroy seconded that with their collective amen's.

"I saw those guys in concert not long ago," Jane said in a hushed voice as she rested her hand on her daughter's head. Candace had crawled into her lap an hour earlier and fell asleep. "They were really good. You wouldn't know they'd had those kinds of issues before they... you know, got it right with God."

"When God does His healing work," Faith said with a smile, "He finishes it, if we let Him."

"Charlie and his father are very close now." Mike added, collecting the used mugs in the living room. "They have an incredible relationship, and even though it's hard for his father to rely on Charlie as much as he does, you can see the love they have for each other."

"And Leroy?" Jane prompted.

"He's dating a lovely young woman from the church. She plays classical guitar." Faith smiled. "If they marry and have kids, we won't need another guitar player for years."

Jane laughed quietly as she smoothed her hand over her daughter's long blonde hair. "Well, I guess it's late. I'm sure you want to get your own kids into bed."

Faith caught Mike's eye and winked.

"Are you sure you want to leave now? We have one more story we could manage to stay awake long enough to tell you."

"Yes, please!" Jane's face lit up with enthusiasm. "And then I promise to pack up my brats and get out of your way."

"It's been a pleasure having you visit," Faith assured her. "Now, where to begin…"

Total Reconciliation

Chapter One

"God has everything under control," Chuck told his wife as he gripped the steering wheel. They remained in the parking lot of the hospital long after the doctor had given him the diagnosis.

"I know, honey." Melanie reached across the space between them, touching his leg. The tears in her green eyes belied the gentle smile on her face. "That doesn't mean I like the diagnosis."

"God hasn't given up on me." Chuck closed his eyes, as another wave of exhaustion drained more of his strength. "He could heal me. We might have another fifty years together."

"Of course." She nodded, fully aware of what her husband was doing. Chuck didn't want her to worry if God didn't make a miracle happen. "Why don't we go home? You look like you could use a nap."

"And you'll make some calls," he teased her. After five years of marriage, his wife's reaction to any sort of crisis was predictable. She'd activate their church's prayer line, and he adored her for her faith in their Lord and Savior.

Chuck started the car, paid the parking lot toll and headed home. He wouldn't argue. A nap sounded like a good idea; he'd slept through the past three months before the doctor finally diagnosed his exhaustion.

Cancer.

What a hideous word, Chuck gritted his teeth. To him, it meant gross weight loss, weakness, and death. Of course the treatment would probably have been as bad, what with constant nausea, hair loss, and total annihilation of the immune system.

But he would have grabbed at a chance for treatment. However, the doctor made it clear that his type of cancer was rare, deadly, and untreatable. Six weeks. That's all the time he had left with his wife.

Six weeks.

Chuck couldn't get his head around that fact. The irony was, as a teenager, he'd courted danger with the intention of not getting out of his antics alive. He rode motorcycles at top speed, and played with guns.

All because his own father had committed suicide.

"Do you remember that man in our church?" Melanie asked, dabbing at her eyes with a tissue she'd found in her purse. "The doctor only gave him six months, but God healed him."

"Yes, I remember." He nodded. He'd let her talk about the miracles God had performed in others, if it made her feel better.

"And then there was that little girl whose kidneys were shutting down. The church prayed when it looked like she wouldn't survive the night but God brought her through."

"Yes, I remember."

"That can be you, Chuck." She squeezed his leg, offering comfort. "We can't give up hope."

"I never said I gave up," he pointed out.

They didn't talk again until they walked into their house. They had a nice home, Chuck thought as if suddenly seeing the place for the first time. Two-storey, hard wood floors, every room had its own color scheme, it was tidy, and smelled like cinnamon.

Yep, he'd been blessed and most days he'd never even recognized that fact.

"Do you want me to come upstairs with you?" she asked as he shrugged out of his jacket. Melanie took it and hung it up for him. "I could stay with you until you fall asleep."

"No." He shook his head. "You go ahead and make your phone calls. I'll be alright."

"Okay."

Even as she said it, he knew she'd be up to check on him after she'd finished with the phone.

Chuck entered their bedroom. The blinds were pulled to about the half way point, the bed was made. There wasn't a speck of dust on the furniture. God had truly blessed him with a good wife, he thought as he sat down on his side of the bed. It would devastate her if he didn't get better. Even though he'd done some horrible things in his past, before he'd given his life to the Lord, Melanie never once threw them in his face. She never told him he was a loser. And she never withheld her love when he didn't do what she wanted, like taking out the trash.

Chuck stretched out on the flower-patterned bedspread and closed his eyes, but didn't immediately fall asleep. He prayed first.

"Lord, I don't know why You decided now was the time to let me get sick. Your Word tells me Your timing is always perfect, but in my eyes that doesn't seem the case." He suddenly grinned as peace spread through him. "And yet You kept me from dying when I was a kid, lost in my sins. If You'd have taken my life then I'd never have known You, never have been blessed with a wife like Melanie, and certainly wouldn't have a chance to get to Heaven."

He released the breath he'd been holding for what seemed like months.

"I won't argue with You, Lord," he said, surrendering completely. "Whatever Your plans are for me, let them bring glory and honor to You. And please, comfort Melanie. Give her that peace that only You can give. The kind that strengthens us when we don't have any will to fight left in us."

With those words on his lips, Chuck fell asleep.

"Oh, Melanie, I'm so sorry."

Melanie heard Faith sob over the phone. That was a human reaction, she acknowledged silently. The Bible said we're supposed to bear one another burdens, to weep when our blood bought family weeps, and to laugh when they laugh. Somehow hearing her best friend react in such an emotional way comforted her. She wasn't alone in her grief.

"Where is Chuck now?" Faith asked, sniffing.

"He's resting," Melanie said. "But I'm sure he's doing some soul searching and praying. I know I am."

"Would you like company? I can be there in ten minutes," Faith said.

"No. I'm okay right now," Melanie replied. "Maybe it hasn't hit me, yet I think God has been preparing my heart for this news for a while. I just wanted to call and get the prayer line going." She smiled through the tears coursing down her cheeks. "But that doesn't mean I won't call and ask you to come babysit me when I'm having a meltdown."

"I'm here for you, sister," Faith said. "We all are. And once the pastor hears about this he'll be on your doorstep."

"Chuck will appreciate that."

They talked for a few more minutes before hanging up. Despite the disastrous news of the day, Melanie felt strangely buoyed in her spirit. After putting a chicken in the oven to bake, she headed up the stairs to check on her husband.

Lately, his appetite had waned, but she had to make sure he ate something to keep what little strength he had left.

The door was partially closed; she pushed it open and peeked in. Chuck was asleep on his back. The lines of his face had deepened over the past few months, given the degree of his illness and the massive amount of weight he'd lost. Fifty pounds to some people might not seem a whole lot, but it was significant for a man as slight as Chuck.

She crossed the room to her side of the bed, and gently leaned back against her pillow. When she touched his chest, his face turned to her in his sleep. It struck her just how frail he looked.

"Please, God," she whispered, "I know Your ways are so much higher than ours, and we don't understand Your purposes a lot of times, but please, spare him. But only if it's Your will."

It was the hardest thing she'd ever prayed.

Chapter Two

[Thirty Years Ago]

Fifteen year old Chuck sat on the back step of his house, making lines in the dirt with a stick he'd found. Today they'd buried his oldest brother. Last week it'd been his father. Would it be him next?

Tormented by the memories of seeing two of his family members in coffins, he tossed the stick away and covered his face with his hands. Tears of rage weren't far behind the memories, but he kept them at bay. Not long ago his other brother had tried to take his own life but the police arrived in time to give him CPR.

Other families inherited the ability to play baseball or the piano, but not his, Chuck thought as rage built inside him. Not his. They'd inherited the compulsion to hang a noose in the garage and stick their necks in it.

If his mother wasn't watching him like a hawk on guard at a chicken coop, he'd consider giving it a go himself. What kind of a life could he have if his own father couldn't stand to live?

"Hey Chuck." One of the neighborhood boys pushed through the bushes along the side of his family's property and greeted him with a wide grin as if nothing serious had happened today. "Thought you might like to hang out with me and the guys. We got some plans and figured you'd have some free time on your hands."

Chuck opened his mouth to tell him off. Didn't he know his brother was dead? But then he shrugged. Doing something other than sitting around and crying like a baby seemed like a better option.

"Yeah, why not?" He stood up and followed the boy back through the bushes.

What the gang of fifteen year olds planned to do wasn't above the law; not that Chuck expected them to act like angels. They were known for stealing anything they came in contact with that wasn't glued, nailed, or chained down. And they'd mastered the art of pick pocketing.

Chuck's father had warned him to stay away from these boys, but where was his dad when he needed him? Dead. One side of Chuck's mouth pressed into his cheek at the irony. Without his father around, he could pretty much do whatever he wanted.

That was the logic he'd use for the next ten years.

By the time he turned nineteen, Chuck knew how to rob a man while asking for directions, how to break into a car and steal the stereo system, and how to case a neighborhood.

He made the bulk of his living by breaking and entering. He watched covertly whenever people left their homes carrying suitcases. He'd give it a day, notice if anyone watered the house plants, checked the mail, or cared for the family pets. When it was obvious no one did, he'd get in through a window. With the help of his buddies, he'd haul away electronics, jewelry, and anything else to make it worth his while.

It was too risky to sell to a pawn shop, so he and his gang made sales on the street to people in other cities who didn't mind buying televisions out of the trunk of a car.

"Okay, guys." Ralph, one of Chuck's friends, rounded up his boys at the local coffee shop and planned out the next big heist. "This is going to be our biggest haul yet. I know for a fact that the house we've been drooling over for the past three months is going on the market."

"I don't want to buy a house," one of the other boys said.

"Will you listen to me," Ralph snapped. "There's going to be an open house. Chuck, you'll go. And when you can, pretend to check out one of the bedrooms. Crack open a window, so we can get in the next night."

"Won't they get suspicious of a kid going in there and looking around?" Chuck asked.

"That's why you're going to wear a business suit and get your hair cut," Ralph said, grinning. "You're not going alone either. My sister will be with you."

"Which one?" Chuck asked, hoping it'd be Ralph's youngest sister Maryanne. She had a smart mouth but she was pretty.

"Joan."

"What?" Of all Ralph's sisters, Joan was the last one Chuck wanted to be seen with. At twenty four, she was beautiful but also six months pregnant, and very obviously so.

"You two are going to look like a married couple," Ralph explained. "No one would ever expect a young married couple, expecting their first brat, to be casing a house. It's perfect."

It was a good plan. Ralph was a great leader who knew how to think. That was the main reason they'd never been caught.

The next day, Chuck and Joan drove to the open house. Wearing their finest clothes, they could have passed as a happily married couple looking for a home to raise a family.

"You're tie is crooked," Joan said, reaching up to straighten it as they stood on the sidewalk. "There, much better." She pressed her palms to his chest and looked up into his face. "You clean up pretty good."

"You too." Chuck smiled appreciatively at her. Of course, Ralph promised her a cut in the take. With a kid on the way, she needed a little financial help.

"Can I hold on to your arm?" she asked. "I feel like I'm having an elephant instead of a baby. And my back is killing me."

Chuck let her lean against him, and despite her pregnant state she didn't seem to weigh much. He wondered if she ate enough to sustain her and the baby. However, the moment they entered the house he forgot about her.

The house was everything Chuck expected it to be. From the stereo system and televisions to the furniture, the house was in showroom condition. Too bad they didn't deal with sofas and dining room sets, he lamented for a moment until they continued up the stairs to view the bedrooms.

The house boasted two complete bathrooms on the second floor, and four fully furnished bedrooms decked out in more of the fancy fixtures. Each room also had its very own television and sound system. He was drooling by the time they reached the master bedroom.

The mahogany furniture, pieces reminiscent of the renaissance era—Chuck knew that much from earlier hauls— filled the rooms. The temptation to check out the contents of each wardrobe was nearly his undoing but Joan kept him firmly by her side.

"Later," she hissed low enough for him to hear and no one else. "I'm going to pretend I need to use the bathroom. If the window is big enough, I'll wedge it open."

She had the same foresight as her brother, Chuck realized impressed. If she hadn't been pregnant, he'd have asked her out on a date.

Ten minutes later, they were back in the car heading to Ralph's apartment. "We make a good pair," Joan said, slanting a playful glance Chuck's way.

"Don't you mean trio?" Chuck asked, dropping his gaze to her swollen belly.

"Yeah, I guess I do." She laughed good-humouredly. "I always liked you, Chuck."

He turned a frown on her before watching the road again. He hadn't expected that admission from her.

"Maybe when this is all done, we could get married." She rubbed her belly, and Chuck wondered if she'd said it out of desperation, wanting to give her child a father.

"I'm just a kid myself," he pointed out.

"I was drinking before I turned twelve," she said, as if that qualified a child for adulthood. "You're what, twenty?"

"Nineteen. You're five years older than me."

"Five years, what's that?" She gave a one shoulder shrug.

"What about the other guys your brother hangs around with?"

"I don't like them," she said. "They're stupid. But not you. You got brains. You're going places. What you need is direction, and I can give you that."

"Why don't we just see what happens tonight before we make any life changing decisions?" Chuck said, side stepping the subject.

"Sure." She sent him a cheeky smile. "But that doesn't mean I'll forget."

Chapter Three

Chuck and his buddies had the best haul of their careers that night. It took two cars to carry away sound systems, televisions, and a few other articles that would bring in a lot of money. Then they split up and headed in two different directions to throw off the police. Chuck went with Ralph. They ended up three hundred miles away from the town, hoping it'd give them an alibi just in case someone was able to figure out who was behind the theft.

After eating at a diner, they booked into a motel and played a game of cards, killing time until they'd meet up with the rest of the gang and decide where to see the goods. However, before they could savor their victory, a squad car pulled up outside the rented room and flashed their squad lights.

"How'd they find out?" Ralph demanded, peeking under a corner of the filthy curtains.

Chuck's mind went blank. They hadn't left any clues behind, no finger prints, nothing. However, the police had warrants for their arrest for the robbery.

While sitting in the jail cell, waiting for their lawyer, they found out what had alerted the police. The other guys, who'd been in on the heist with them, weren't smart enough to keep attention off them. Their reckless speeding had them pulled over not two miles from the robbery.

Ron, one of the new guys in the gang, afraid of being charged with breaking and entering and theft, spilled everything to the officer. The driver tried to explain away the stolen goods, saying they were in the process of moving, which would explain the stereo in the back seat. But Ron confessed, saying he thought he was helping his buddies move and didn't know they were actually robbing a house until afterwards.

The police seemed sympathetic, and thinking he'd gained their friendship, Ron went on to tell them exactly where they could find the rest of the stolen goods.

"I never did trust that guy," Ralph said, the glint in his eyes murderous.

Chuck might have felt sorry for what was going to happen to the snitch when Ralph got out of jail, but he too was facing prison time and his sympathies were more for himself than anyone else.

However, things didn't work out the way he thought they would. When Chuck and Ralph were led to the courtroom for their hearing, Joan was there waiting. He wasn't surprised, Ralph was her brother and he'd been looking after her.

What did surprise Chuck was when his assigned lawyer mentioned him having a fiancée and that he'd only gotten mixed up with the gang on account of the baby and not having enough money to care for it.

"Considering every child needs their father," the judge said, looking down his nose at Chuck, "I'm going to grant you probation for one year. Should you keep away from illegal activities, you won't face prison time. I encourage you to find a job and take care of your family, Mr. Benson."

That was it. Bemused, he let Joan lead him from the courthouse while she looked every bit the doting fiancée.

"Why'd you do that?" he asked as she drove them back to their home town.

"You heard the judge." She sent him a mischievous grin that he'd come to expect from her. "Every child needs their father."

They were married two weeks later by the justice of the peace and moved into their own apartment. It didn't take long for them to bypass domestic bliss. She wasn't much of a house keeper, preferring to watch television to looking after the household. When he finished up his shift for the day at the local café, he had to get his own supper. And she complained constantly about his low paying job.

By the time the baby arrived, Chuck knew he and Joan didn't stand a chance to make things work out between them. By Christmas, she packed up her little girl and moved back with her parents.

His probation over, and nothing left for his future than his dead-end jobs waiting tables at restaurants, Chuck decided it was time to move onto more exciting things and better pay.

It wasn't difficult to find trouble. Chuck found his kind of people at the pool hall.

"You used to work with Ralph," John, the co-owner of the hall said, as he leaned over the table to make a shot.

"Yeah." Chuck drank slowly from his beer can as he watched John and his friend shoot pool.

"You looking for work?"

"I got a job." Chuck finished his beer and dropped it into a nearby garbage can.

"I don't mean nine to five," John clarified. "I'm talking big bucks."

"I'm listening," Chuck said, crossing his arms over his chest.

"How good are you at knocking over convenience stores?" John asked.

"Never done it," Chuck said. "But I'm a fast learner."

"Good." John straightened up and grinned. "Good."

It took a week of planning. John was meticulous with the details and Chuck liked his professionalism. What he balked at was murder.

"The clerk dies before they can pull the alarm," John said as they shared a pizza at his home. "We don't leave any witnesses. I don't plan on spending time in the slammer."

Chuck didn't say anything. If he argued at this point he suspected John wouldn't have any compunction about getting rid of him. Instead, he decided he'd do his best to keep any one from getting hurt while they cleaned out the cash register and anything else they could get their hands on.

The night of the robbery, Chuck was given his first hand gun. He hated the cold metal and equally cold look in John's eyes.

"Not scared are you, Chuck?" John asked, his tone edging on a taunt.

"Nope." And he wasn't. What did he have to live for anyway? His marriage had ended in divorce, and he never got to see the kid. If he died tonight, no big deal. If he ended up murdered in prison no big loss either. Whichever way he looked, the outcome remained the same: death. And the faster the better.

When Chuck stood before the judge again the following day it was with a sense of déjà vu. Chuck kept his head down. The attempted robbery had been a disaster. The store clerk hid behind the bullet proof wall and called 9-1-1, and locked the doors behind them in attempt to keep them locked in until the police arrived.

John managed to bust his way out through the exit, but it didn't take long for the authorities to pick him up. Chuck had remained in the store. He'd opened a bag of chips and a bottle of pop and waited nonchalantly.

The judge sentenced him to twelve and a half years for his part in the armed robbery. Chuck stood in his orange prison uniform facing the judge and when asked if he had anything to say, his comment had been a simple, "No, sir."

This had to be the end of things for him, Chuck silently hoped as the guard led him away from the court room. He was tired. Tired of living. Tired of not having a future, and tired of hating himself.

Chapter Four

The day Chuck was released from his twelve year stint in prison, he felt old and worn out. He decided against taking a cab into town choosing instead to walk. It was the first time he could enjoy the sunshine and fresh air without being watched. Even a simple thing like kicking rocks brought a smile to his face.

He'd seen a lot while behind bars. Things that aged a man before his time. That didn't include the multiple prison riots he'd survived, twelve of Chuck's friends were dead, including John, his former buddy who'd talked him into holding up the convenience store a long time ago. He'd been one of the guys behind last year's riot.

The prison had gone into immediate lockdown, no questions asked. All the prisoners lost privileges for nearly six months. And because Chuck had known some of the guys who'd instigated the violence, he'd spent three months in the hole. Guilty by association.

That was the closest he'd ever come to death. Naked, no contact with anyone, nothing to do but live with your memories. And his weren't particularly heartwarming.

He kept thinking about his dad. His brother. Chuck cursed them for taking their lives when they had so much to live for, family being at the top of the list. What could have been so awful they couldn't endure living? What kind of life Chuck might have had if his father hadn't been a selfish man?

The rage that came on the heels of his thoughts spurred him into picking up the pace. He didn't expect answers to those questions, so he'd have to live with them and his bitterness.

Chuck spent his first night of freedom on a park bench, using newspapers for a cover, and looking exactly what he was: a bum.

"Is that you, Chuck?"

Chuck slowly opened his eyes and looked up into a familiar face. Ralph.

"Man, I haven't seen you in ages," Ralph said, holding out his hand. "What are you doing here?"

"Fresh out of prison," Chuck said, rubbing his eyes, trying to work the haze out of them.

"No kidding." Ralph stepped back, crossed his arms over his chest. "I got out ten years back. Didn't have a pregnant fiancée giving a sob story to get me paroled." There was no missing the sarcasm in his voice.

"That was a mistake," Chuck mumbled, sitting up. "What ever happened to Joan?"

"Got married again to some loser. You should see her girl, pretty little thing. Blonde, blue eyed. She could have passed for yours."

The words stung. For the first time in years, Chuck regretted the decisions he'd made. Maybe if he'd tried, he could have worked things out with Joan, and they could have raised the little girl together. But he'd been selfish, just like his father.

"Have you got no place to go?" Ralph asked, continuing to talk when Chuck didn't speak.

"What you see." Chuck patted the bench.

"Why don't you come back to my house? The wife can cook you a good meal, and we can talk business."

Chuck knew what kind of business Ralph had on his mind. Some things never changed. However, he wasn't going to turn down a home cooked meal.

"That was delicious," Chuck said after sopping up the last of the chicken gravy on his plate with a slice of homemade bread. "Thank you."

"Stick around and she'll put some meat on those scrawny bones of yours," Ralph said with a chuckle.

"Might take you up on that," Chuck said, half serious.

"Now, why don't we take our beer and go into the living room and reminisce?"

Chuck followed his old pal, sat down on the sofa, and took a long drink of his beer.

"I heard you'd had a hand in holding up that convenience store a few years back," Ralph said. "Could I interest you in another one?"

"Your contacts didn't tell you everything, obviously," Chuck said. "I got sent to prison for it."

"Well, let's say this time you don't get caught?"

Chuck didn't say yes but he didn't say no either. What did he have to lose? There wasn't anything or anyone waiting for him outside of prison. And two nights later, he stood at the cash register of a local convenience store stuffing cigarettes into his pocket while Ralph pointed a gun in the terrified clerk's face.

When he went back to the motel room, alone this time, paid for by the convenience store he'd robbed, Chuck couldn't settle down. He couldn't sleep, the television didn't interest him, and he didn't have cards to play solitaire.

Robbing the store hadn't been a highlight of his life. In fact, he knew he'd never forget the look of terror in the young woman's face as Ralph leveled a gun on her. What if something had happened? If Ralph had been over eager, and pulled the trigger by accident? What if…

Desperate to take his mind off his thoughts, he rummaged through the side table drawer. Sometimes people forgot magazines, or books. However, his search produced a Bible.

Any other time, he'd have tossed the Bible back in the drawer and shut it, but not this time. In his hands, it opened to a passage which had already been underlined in blue ink.

"He whom the Son sets free is free indeed." He read the words out loud, over and over until they filled his head and his heart and his room. Chuck didn't understand exactly what they'd meant but they stirred up hope in his heart.

"God, if there's a chance for me," Chuck prayed for the first time in his life, "Please, show me."

Chuck woke the next morning on top of the bedspread, completely dressed in the same clothes he'd worn the night before. The motel Bible he clutched to his chest like it was a teddy bear.

Groaning, he rolled to the side of the bed and sat up holding the Bible. In the process of planning out his day, he remembered the date. And that it was the anniversary of his father's suicide.

Though he'd never visited his father's gravesite before, Chuck suddenly felt an overwhelming need to go.

The cemetery was on the outskirts of his hometown, where most of the town's dead rested. Not that his father deserved to rest in peace, Chuck thought as he gritted his teeth. Mindful of the other graves, he carefully made his way across the tended grass until he found his father's site.

The marker was a simple cross bearing his father's name and date of his birth and death. There was no mention of his suicide. That was okay with Chuck, no sense in airing dirty laundry for future generations to see.

"Well Dad," he said, clasping his hands together in front of him respectfully and looking down at the marker. "What do you think of your boy? He's done a few years in jail and pretty much messed up his life. Thanks to you and your selfish little choice to put a noose around your neck. Tell me, what were you thinking? I'd really like to know."

The slamming of car doors snapped Chuck out of his tirade. Before he could beat a hasty retreat, the couple walking into the cemetery stopped his exit.

"Is that you, Chuck?" The heavy set woman with thick dark hair and glasses addressed him.

It was the second time in two weeks someone asked him that question. For a man who pretty much kept to himself he seemed to be popular lately.

"Well?" The woman stepped closer to him and gave him a hug. "Don't you know me?" she asked when she finally released him.

The minute she said that, he knew. Her face might be older, and a few more pounds added to her waistline, but he knew.

"Aunt Mabel."

She'd been his favorite aunt. When he was a kid, she never forgot his birthday, had sent him Christmas presents, and gave him money whenever she stopped in to visit his family.

"What have you been up to all this time, Chuck?" she asked, rubbing his arms as her suspiciously moist eyes continued to look him over as if she couldn't believe she was talking to him.

Chuck hated to tell her but figured he might as well be honest.

"I've been in prison, Aunt Mabel."

"Oh, you poor boy. I never knew."

"Yeah, Mom was too embarrassed to tell anyone." That was an understatement. Anytime anyone asked, his mother always said the same thing; Chuck was doing good, moved to Canada with his high paying job as a chartered accountant.

"You've never met my husband," she said, as if remembering the man standing not too far from them. "This is my nephew, Chuck. Chuck, this is George." Beneath her gaze, the two men shook hands. "He's a retired police officer, my George."

Chuck dropped the man's hand as if it suddenly scorched him.

"Don't be silly, Chuck," she scolded. "We're not here to cause you trouble. In fact, now that I've found you I want you to come home with us."

It was the last thing Chuck wanted; to associate with a retired officer. And yet the appeal in his favorite aunt's eyes was his undoing.

By that evening, his aunt had him moved in with them until he found a job and could afford his own place. He'd even gone to church with them the following Sunday. The pastor preached on God being in control no matter what the circumstances in your life. Just when you think you have nothing to live for, God had a plan. Because he whom the Son set free was free indeed!

Chuck recognized the words as those he'd read in the Bible back in the motel room the night following the robbery. Had God heard his cry?

"God hears every cry, my friend," the pastor went on to say, echoing Chuck's thoughts. "If you want the peace and security you've been looking for all your life, come to the altar tonight and surrender to His will for you."

He didn't realize he was crying until Aunt Mabel touched his arm.

"Chuck?" she whispered. "D you want to go forward?"

He nodded wordlessly.

"Do you want me to go with you?"

He nodded again. Moments later, he and his aunt had joined the small crowd gathered around the altar. But Chuck knew, in his heart, had he been the only one, he still would have gone.

That night, after confessing his sins, Chuck was a brand new man. The pastor stepped down to talk with each new convert, and Chuck ended up telling him about his part in the robbery.

With no one pressuring him, the next morning, Chuck turned himself into the police for his part in robbing the convenience store. He was sentenced to one year in prison, and for his exemplary behavior, he was paroled in less than eight months.

During his time in prison, he studied his Bible and attended church services. And after his release, he'd met Melanie at Aunt Mabel's church. They married the following summer.

Chuck had never known just how wonderful life could be. His only regret was that his father and brother wouldn't get the chance to find out for themselves.

Chapter Five

"Chuck? I know you're awake."

Melanie's soft voice reached his ears and he slowly opened his eyes. He turned and looked into her face, regretting the sorrow he found there.

"What were you thinking about, honey?" she asked, rubbing his hand as she sat beside him.

He'd been admitted to the hospital a month ago, and had since been moved to palliative care. It was like a motel room, with a small kitchenette, sofa and arm chair, and television. The only thing that set it apart from an actual motel was the I.V. pole hooked up to his arm.

"I was remembering what the Lord took me out of," he said. "How He blessed me with you and the people He'd brought into my life through the church."

"Oh." She brought his hand to her lips, and he felt her tears on his skin.

"Don't be sad, Mel," he urged. "God spoke to me and said my death is like the birthing process, as contradictory as that may seem. He's waiting to catch me when my spirit enters Heaven, the way a doctor catches a baby at the end of its mother's labor. I'm going home."

"I'm not sad, honey," she said, sniffing and smiling through the tears. "I'm envious. I wish I were going with you."

"I'll be waiting," he told her, pressing her cool hands to his face. "Jesus and I will be waiting for you when you come home."

They looked up when someone softly knocked on the door.

"It's just us," Faith said, peaking around the corner. "Is this a bad time?"

"Never for you," Chuck said, struggling to sit up.

"We brought a surprise." Faith smiled as if anticipating his reaction.

"Surprise." A blonde woman threw her arms wide and gave him a huge grin.

"Charlotte." Chuck immediately recognized her. He waved her forward for a hug. "You've grown into quite a young lady," he said, touching her long hair.

"Thank you, Dad."

Chuck started at that, the same he did every time she called him that.

After he'd given his life to Christ, he'd gotten in touch with Joan. He discovered that she was divorced again and having it rough financially. When he got out of jail, he got a decent job, thanks to Pastor Haden and Harry Emerson Senior, and he was able to send money to Joan and Charlotte to get them through each month.

After he'd started sending the checks, Charlotte had made a point of meeting him. He remembered her only as a crying baby, but they quickly got over their shyness of each other and she saw the way he tried to live his life with integrity. She knew his history from the stories her Uncle Ralph and her mother had told her, but she got to see for herself the kind of man he'd grown into. And it wasn't too long before she went to church with him and Melanie. And a couple weeks later she bent her knees at the altar and surrendered her life to God.

"I should have come sooner," she whispered.

"It's great to see you now," Chuck told her with a shaky smile. Holding her hand and looking up into her dear face brought tears to his eyes. She couldn't have been more special to him than if she'd been his blood child.

For the next twenty minutes, the small group had a quiet conversation. Each one telling Chuck how blessed they were to have known him, and the impact he'd made in their lives.

"And to think," he said, awed as he looked at the dear faces around him, "God took a man who wanted to die and gave him every reason to live. And now I will, for eternity."

"You'd never know," Faith said as Jane readied her children to leave, "Chuck, a man who'd spent so much time in prison, had so much love and compassion to give."

"How is he doing?" Jane asked, buttoning her daughter's sweater against the chilly evening.

"He's still in palliative care." Mike put his arm around Faith's shoulders and she leaned into his side. "He's very weak, but as his body fails his spirit grows stronger."

"I wish I'd had a chance to know him," Jane said, her voice filled with regret. "Could I ask a question?"

"Go ahead." Faith nodded.

"If…if anything…if he," Jane faltered. "If Chuck dies, could I go to the funeral with you?"

"Absolutely. Chuck has every detail all planned out. He wants it to be a celebration of the life God had given him."

A single tear trailed down Jane's face. "Somehow, that's what I expected to hear you say."

Epilogue

[One Month Later]

The church was filled to capacity as Chuck's life was celebrated. Jane and her family sat down next to Mike and Faith and the boys. After the evening she'd spent with her friends and hearing the life changing stories, Jane had gone home and repeated them to her husband.

He'd listened with avid interest and ever since that night, they'd talked about God whenever they got together. There hadn't been any more arguments between them, as their interest turned to God and the Bible.

Now here they sat together, a united front. She turned her face up to his and they shared a secret smile. This was their first time in her friends' church. And she had a feeling it wasn't going to be the last.

She looked down at the program in her hand and smiled as she recognized the names of the people involved in the funeral service, and being able to put faces to those names.

Leroy and Charlie played a blues style rendition of Amazing Grace, the one Chuck personally requested, Harry Emerson Senior gave his eulogy focusing mainly on the man God made of him, Jo-Jo sang a solo. Tommy, Harry Junior, David and Paul Emerson, Wayne Young, and Mike were pallbearers, and Pastor Haden gave the salvation message that Chuck wanted preached to the fifteen hundred plus congregation.

There wasn't a dry eye in the church that spring afternoon. Chuck obviously meant a lot to this family.

After the funeral, Jane's son, Pete, strolled over to Chuck's widow, Melanie, and hugged her; a complete stranger. He'd always been the most sensitive of her children.

"I'm sorry God had to take Mr. Chuck away from you," he said with child-like sincerity.

"Don't be sorry, honey," Melanie said, rubbing his back. "He's gone to be with Jesus. And one day I'll go there too. What about you?"

"The preacher said to go to Heaven I have to ask Jesus in my heart," Pete said.

Faith and Jane smiled at each other through their tears as it became obvious Jane's boy had been listening.